Welcome Thieves

WELCOME THIEVES

stories

SEAN BEAUDOIN

ALGONQUIN BOOKS OF CHAPEL HILL 2016

Published by
ALGONQUIN BOOKS OF CHAPEL HILL
Post Office Box 2225
Chapel Hill, North Carolina 27515-2225

a division of
WORKMAN PUBLISHING
225 Varick Street
New York, New York 10014

This is a work of fiction. While, as in all fiction, the literary
perceptions and insights are based on experience, all names,
characters, places, and incidents either are products of the
author's imagination or are used fictitiously.

Library of Congress Cataloging-in-Publication Data
Beaudoin, Sean.
[Short stories. Selections]
Welcome thieves : stories / by Sean Beaudoin.
pages ; cm
ISBN 978-1-61620-457-0
I. Title.
PS3602.E2634A6 2016
813'.6—dc23   2015022973

10 9 8 7 6 5 4 3 2 1
First Edition

To Cathy, who for fifteen years
has held my hand, heart,
and cliché in equal measure.

Contents

The following stories have appeared elsewhere, often in different form. "Nick in Nine (9) Movements" in *Litro Magazine*. "Hey Monkey Chow" in *Bat City Review*. "D.C. Metro" in *The Nervous Breakdown*. "All Dreams Are Night Dreams" in *Narrative Magazine*. "And Now Let's Have Some Fun" in *Identity Theory*. "Tiffany Marzano's Got a Record" in *Redivide*r. "Comedy Hour" in *Another Chicago Magazine*. "Exposure" in *Instant City*. "Welcome Thieves" in *Glimmer Train*.

Nick in Nine (9) Movements

Nick becomes Nikki, Duff was always Duff. They start playing in ninth grade because Duff's stepbrother is in a band called Lewinsky Rescue and sometimes the stepbrother gets laid, so why not? But mostly they drink and wear tube socks and have a van. It's fun. They come up with a name, Torrentials, and play hardcore, which is not punk and so involves constantly correcting people. Duff says, "Hardcore is to a pickax what punk is to lipstick."

There are some fights.

Duff wears an earring and a Gibson SG, has natural rhythm and easy chops. Shaves his head. Kicks who needs kicking. Nikki's too pretty to pretend that everything sucks, but tries. Gets an E-string tattoo, tags deli Dumpsters, parties with that drummer with the infected toe. Still, he's always a beat behind, a measure off, up in his room running scales every second he's not being yelled at by the guy who isn't Dad but moved in anyway.

Some equipment must be acquired.

Duff says they should rip off a dance band. Or cut a hole in the roof of Kane's Guitars, lower a rope, and haul up Johnny Ramone's Strat. "Good idea, tier boss," Nikki says, gets two jobs, quits two jobs, finally snags an off-brand bass on lay-away. No label, no logo, made in Seoul. It's called "Bass." The plastic case is lined with fake pink fur that Duff says smells like pussy, which makes Nikki think Duff was lying about all those cheerleaders because it smells nothing like pussy and Nikki would know since he's been hanging out at Dana Gold-stein's for months, especially on Sunday nights when both her parents work and they can listen to Agnostic Front on the futon.

Some glue is sniffed.

Torrentials play their first show, eight bands all ages mosh pits low ceilings. Sharpie Xs and studded belts. Aiming for Fugazi while pretending not to. But it works. The skinheads gob less than usual, say, *Eh, yer okay.* The girls in leather skirts nod in time to the beat, in time to each other, gaze over Wayfarers at Nikki's low rumble.

Some gas is huffed.

The next day Duff decides he doesn't like their name any-more, wants to change to November Regions. Nikki thinks November Regions is the lamest fucking name in the history of lame fucking names.

It sounds like a tampon commercial.

It sounds like a free U2 download.

Which means it's perfect, since Nikki secretly wants to be huge. Wants to bend over like Green Day, get corporate-label famous, a ruinous admission he covers by pretending to be pissed, punches an amp, cracks two knuckles.

Duff apologizes by spray painting the wall of the practice space JESUS LOVES TORRENTIALS. There's an anarchy circle around the A. Nikki has zero clue what anarchy is, or even wants to be. Something about wallet chains and waiters getting more per hour, plus tips. The band rounds out. A kid named Drew takes over drums, too good for his own good, runs jazz patterns in the middle of songs. Max Verbal is lead screamer, has a pompadour, brings sixers of Bud Light and refuses to share. He looks sort of like fat Morrissey, which Nikki knows because he stood lookout while Duff five-fingered *Meat Is Murder* from Record World.

Torrentials have four songs. Three originals, which suck, and a cover of Thompson Twins's "Hold Me Now," which sucks. Max Verbal keeps not sharing his beer and going, "Besides, they're not really even twins." Nikki transposes half a Doobie Brothers just so Verbal can go, "Besides, they're not really even brothers."

They play a couple parties and then a battle of the bands in the school auditorium. After the last song Duff smashes someone else's guitar.

The audience goes crazy.

The kid holds his broken neck, his snapped strings.

Torrentials get the most votes, don't win.

There are some fights.

Prom is for suckers, cap and gown for fags. Except hardcore is about inclusivity and subverting exactly the sort of culture that continues to validate such a word. Fine, Duff says, but insists there's *no way* he's wearing a blue smock, even though he failed chemistry and isn't graduating anyway.

The after-party is lame, so they steal a bottle of wine and climb a tree, take turns reading the first twenty pages of *Tropic of Cancer* by flashlight.

"We gotta hit Europe, yo," Duff says, currently working *yo* and *kid* into every other sentence. "Which means we gotta get paid, kid."

They land the same telemarket job downtown, sit across from each other at a folding table full of dial-up phones, give away free passes to a health club. *You need to get in shape, yo? You like to push iron, kid?* Almost everyone hangs up immediately. Then a girl at the next table figures out how to dial Japan, for a week the whole room calling Tokyo porn lines and asking confused housewives if they're Yakuza, do they want to win a free pinkie finger?

They quit after the second paycheck, sleep three nights at LaGuardia on standby, get seats on a cargo flight with no seats. Nikki couldn't cram Bass into his ancient JanSport, so he bought a harmonica. Not very hardcore but easy to hit the three notes that matter. They land in Berlin, follow the same route Von Clausewitz used to subjugate Poland. Or maybe it was the other direction. Duff grows his hair out. Nikki reaches for a mustache. They stand in the middle of squares and the front of cafés, mostly do blues in E since any other key means drowning in that chordy Dylan routine even Dylan only pulls off half the time.

People stop, watch, walk away.

There are some pigeons.

There is some change.

Duff and Nikki become known as *Der Witzel-something*, which everyone swears is a compliment, but then Klink gets wind and keeps sending Schultz to disperse the crowd. The Euro-hipsters boo, but not too much, since Euro-cops carry machine guns and aren't shy with the boot. In Hamburg, Duff scores a Gretel who gives them a floor and then a week later a ride north. She's on her way to some protest, which basically means smoke pot, wear an Arafat scarf, and chant about not building one thing in favor of building another, better thing.

On the streets of Stockholm a guy in a business suit listens for a minute and then yells, "You know nothing about the blues! Go find another hobby!"

Duff wants to follow the dude, get into it.

"It's bad luck to punch a Swede," Nikki says, which probably isn't true, but keeps them from spending July in Stockholm Rikers.

They've been back four months. Duff's got the clap and three new tattoos. GORE CLUB and PSYCHIC TV and AVAIL. His cousin paints houses on Nantucket, knows a guy who knows a guy. Plus tetracycline. Duff takes Nikki's suitcase more than borrows it, grubs twelve bucks in change, ready to hit the road.

There are some hugs.

Nikki fills out three forms, waits, almost throws away the envelope that says he's won a partial scholarship to a place in Ohio no one has ever heard of. Something State. Dude name of Pell good for a grant. Nikki flags the Greyhound with a Hefty bag full of socks and a well-thumbed Genet. Thirteen hours later a cute girl finally gets on, sits by the window, snores. At school an index card on the message board says CHEAP SAX LESSONS. Nikki buys a 1941 Conn alto for a hundred Pell-bucks and squonks away behind the dorm for weeks before producing a single pure note. It's fantastic. The sax teacher is called Tumast. No last name. Tumast refuses to come on campus, says, "Too many white girls without bras make me nervous." Nikki skates over to his place, more a barn than a shack. More one big room with no kitchen than a place you'd be cool going barefoot. Tumast has three enormous gleaming tenors lined against the wall, tries to sell Nikki the dented one.

After a discussion of John Lee Hooker's mad chops, Tumast nods, says, "You pretty cool for—"

"A white dude?"

"Was gonna say nineteen."

They both laugh.

The phone keeps ringing. Tumast takes off his shirt and pulls yards of Saran Wrap around his waist, says the sweat helps "tighten his shit up." Nikki learns how to play a high C scale, pictures the neighbors as they wince over their frozen dinners, eye their tortured dogs.

Sometimes Tumast scratches at his dandruffy Afro, nods off midsentence.

Nikki figures it's just been a long day.

CLASSES. THAT DRUNK PROFESSOR. Behind the bleachers while football. The library and everything in it not read. Nikki and a little thing named Chelsea, expensive sweaters and wine-dark skin, crashing through cornfields in her dad's Miata. Late nights with cough syrup and candles and Nick Cave, "It's so cool you have the same name," her wide hips and cheap panties, making eggs while she sleeps it off.

He tries out for a few bands, this one too strummy, that one too singer-songwritery. Then a thrash outfit with inverted crosses and eye makeup, afterward the lead screamer going, "Hey, you're not half-bad."

But the dude reminds him too much of Duff.

There is some spoken word.

Someone's half-finished film.

A short story stolen almost entirely from Ray Carver.

Calling Raymond Carver "Ray."

A keg and that guy down the hall who spreads his Kawasaki 750 out on the carpet twice a week.

Fall, winter, spring. Fall again.

That year there was always some prick with a didgeridoo.

DUFF ROLLS INTO TOWN unannounced, three blankets and an '88 LeBaron, moves into the low-slung apartments just off campus everyone calls Crackland. Claims he's signed up for classes but unless there's a master's program in eyeballing eighths, or a PhD in convincing waitresses not to sweat the condom, Nikki doubts it. They jam, Duff slash-fingered and manic, lots of great ideas for liner notes and string arrangements, lots of back slaps and a considered misreading of the circle of fifths.

There are some tantrums.

Duff gets angry when he can't get his amp to "make that crunchy sound like last time." At a party with barrel fires outside he makes a cross with duct tape and two sticks to protest church or some shit, tosses it in, realizes too late he's burning a cross. The Third World Alliance is not pleased. There is an investigation. There is a dark hallway ass-kicking. Duff refuses to shower for three weeks in lieu of filing a written complaint. He calls it a Worker's Action. He says Eugene V. Debs did not wear Ban roll-on. Nikki's friends start calling Duff names like "Smelldolf Hitler" and "Smell Gibson" and "Smells Like Teen Suicide."

But not to his face.

When he finally reunites with soap, there's talk of a duo.

They pull six songs together, try to think of a name.

Nikki likes Pure Candy.

Duff likes the Four Tercels.

Pure Tercel plays two shows, the second in the basement

of a basement, where Duff meets a girl called Agnes. She has a tattoo of a shotgun wound and a birthmark shaped like the Amalfi Coast. Agnes takes Duff by the hand, wants to show him something out back before the next set.

They disappear for the winter.

That spring Nikki graduates with a degree in pulling the graveyard shift at a motel beneath an exit ramp. There's an actual bell on the counter that dings. Once in a while they get a frugal tourist, otherwise it's mainly battered moms and pregnant runaways, plus a guy named Winslow who buys a large black drip and a dozen donuts every morning, sits with his feet dangling over the empty pool. Winslow chuckles, takes a bite, says he's "Killing Myself Fatly with This Song" when anyone asks, which no one does, so he tells whoever walks by, which just makes them walk faster.

There's a cassette deck by the cash box. Nikki plays John Coltrane all shift long, thinks "Alabama" is the saddest melody he's ever heard, plays it over and over louder and louder until dawn, the more trebly and dissonant the better.

Each note a shard of inalterable beauty.

Each note like bug spray for the insane.

THE FAMILY IN 227 never comes back. Nikki gets sent over with gloves and a mop. There's trash everywhere—socks, empties, a bear with all the stuffing hugged out of its neck.

Leaned up against the mini fridge is an old acoustic.

Covered with finger grime and Dead stickers.

It screams hippie chicks with thrift skirts and anklets. It begs for braless fatties to kick off their sandals and spin in the wet grass.

"Anything good?" the manager asks.

"Nope," Nikki says, then rumbles through half a dozen Neil Young in front of the campus Quiznos twice a week. There is a hat. The professor with the too-neat beard drops a twenty and winks. The kind of girls who hang out and listen hang out and listen. The kind of girls who smoke sigh and kill off another Marlboro red.

On a random Tuesday Duff is there, at the edge of the crowd.

Nodding along, or pretending to.

They get beers.

"Where's Agnes?"

"Let the door hit her where the good lord split her."

"She dump you?"

He grins, down a tooth or two. "Yeah, pretty much."

There are some hugs.

Within a week Duff starts a band with a dude named King Ink. They need a bass player. Duff says, "No sweat, I'll vouch for your candy ass."

King Ink calls at midnight, asks Nikki does he want to join.

"You got a name yet?"

"Scrofula," King Ink says.

There's a long pause.

"It's a disease with glandular swellings. Most likely a cousin of tuberculosis."

There's a long pause.

"Listen, you in or not?"

"You haven't heard me play."

"Duff is an astute judge of character."

"That," Nikki says, "is without question the least true thing anyone has ever said aloud."

King Ink insists Scrofula will be the Guns N' Roses of the greater Ohio Valley area. By the second practice it's clear they will never be the Guns N' Roses of the greater Ohio Valley area. King Ink is six-foot-six, wears velvet boots, and has the goatee Rosemary's baby would have grown his freshman year at Sarah Lawrence. Duff says not to worry, the dude is a genius. Besides, once they buy a sampler they'll be playing thousand-seat venues.

Scrofula does six shows, opens two nights for Particle Bored.

And blows them off the stage.

Duff says there's strong label interest. Smoking Goat out of Chicago. Reeves Rimini wants to produce. Duff says King Ink says everyone needs to put up three hundred to cut a demo. Scrofula rehearses the shit out of their setlist, hones it to a tight forty minutes with a killer payoff, a tune Nikki wrote called "Those Chelsea Mournings." After practice they crack beers, load all the gear into the van for the trip to the studio. King Ink takes them each by the shoulders, insists they're on the verge of something.

"Special? No, big. Big? No, huge."

Nikki gets chills down his arms. King Ink orders three large pies to celebrate, splurges on extra pepperoni, takes the van to go pick them up.

And never comes back.

NIKKI DOESN'T TOUCH a guitar for a year, then one day spots a '73 Tele Thinline hanging in a pawnshop, and can't buy it fast enough. The thing so clean it sings. So dirty it's a slut. It takes months to learn that Chet Atkins lick, let alone the James Burton. He writes a dozen new songs, thinks about maybe being frontman for once, get some kids just want to learn their parts, keep their mouths shut.

Memorial Day comes and Nikki agrees to a weekend roadie with day shift clerks he barely knows. Robot, Marcellus, and Gay Don. They camp out one night, hit a titty bar the next, on the way back stop in Columbus to piss. It's hot. Nikki's Replacements T is wet to the shoulder blades. They're at the edge of a campus, a football powerhouse. A strip of dives ten blocks long, beer-soaked carpet and specials in every window, JAEGER TUESDAYS!

"Let's drink," Gay Don says.

"It's not Tuesday," Nikki says.

"Good point," Robot says. "Let's find a museum instead."

"I only have eight bucks," Nikki says.

"Which you should immediately spend on ointment for your vagina," Marcellus says.

By the fourth place they're shit faced.

Gay Don starts telling everyone who'll listen they're a band, mostly because Nikki brought the Thinline in its ratty swing-jazz case, not wanting to leave it in Robot's Camry, which doesn't lock. Gay Don says they're playing the Attic at midnight. A couple girls are like *Oh, really?* not putting much in it. The bartender rolls his eyes, cuts limes. Someone checks the paper. Turns out there really is an Attic, a tiny dump across the river, but it's closed tonight.

"Unannounced show," Marcellus says, swears they'll leave tickets at will call for anyone who buys a round. A few people actually do. Robot runs down the set list for them, how they rock Bon Jovi covers and Robert Johnson covers and John Cage covers. How they crush Black Sabbath covers and Black Flag covers and Black Uhuru covers. Nikki figures as the guitar player his gig is to hang back and be silent and cool and superior, one foot up on the rail. It's worthy of some sort of paper, sociology or physics, how easily the rest fall into unspoken roles. Marcellus lead vocals and acne scars. Robot drums, tatted neck to wrist. Gay Don on eyeliner and bass.

None of them plays an instrument as far as Nikki can tell.

In some ways it's better than actually being in a band.

From bar to bar the story is honed, more believable, less believable. Robot and Gay Don spin the Japanese tour, groupie orgies, failed label deals. People move closer, buy fresh rounds. Nikki concludes that a lie stumbled upon is infinitely more believable than a lie presented. That being a fool allows others to reveal themselves. That the power of belief is redemptive and carries a special allure for the perpetually bored.

On the other hand, it's pretty clear they're being dicks. It's a question of how many drinks are required not to acknowledge it.

"We don't get backup singers on our rider soon, it's time for a new manager," Robot tells an underage girl who claims to sing.

"Bullshit," says a dyed waitress, two sticks of gum and a tray digging into her hip. "Tell me the name of this supergroup again?"

Gay Don looks at Nikki, mouths, *Oh fuck.*

It's worthy of an entirely different paper, this one on the mathematics of sheer dumbassedness, the fact that it hasn't come up yet.

"Yeah, man, what *is* your name?" says the big dude in a Tupac shirt who bought the last round. Doubt flares. Conversations stop. There are maybe twenty people in the bar, a group of sports guys with backward caps and team sweatshirts, a few townies and metal dudes wristing foosball. Nikki can feel an undertow, an ugly gravity, an inevitable beat down coming. For some reason the entire room turns to him as he leans on the guitar case with half a glass of someone else's beer.

"We are Crustimony Proseedcake."

It's the first thing that pops into his head. *The Tao of Pooh* had been on the nightstand of the last girl he hooked up with, a yoga teacher who shot a killer game of nine ball. He'd read a few pages while she was in the shower.

There's a lengthy silence.

Sun blares under the half-door, causes the rubber floor mats to steam.

And then Robot smashes a bottle on his forehead, yells, "Pro-fucking-*seed*-cake!'"

Solved.

Out come the vodka shots. Out come the backslaps and air jamming. Every ten minutes someone new walks in and the entire bar yells, "Pro-*seed*-cake!"

Crustimony hits two more spots, adds groupies and acolytes and believers and skeptics and marketing majors and homeless artists and lab assistants and lacrosse team wingers by the block. It's late afternoon. Everyone is very drunk. Nikki has just been in the bathroom with a girl who had horrible breath and after a minute said, *No no no, my breath*, and pushed him away, stumbling back to where her friends sat on a broken Ping-Pong table.

The music pounds and people dance and then it's time to leave, everyone promising to come see them that night.

"Sound check at ten sharp, y'all," Robot says, one last salute at the door.

All the way back to the car they laugh, barely able to stand. It's a running guy hug, a shoulder-squeezing, unbalanced affair. They punch and slap and checklist through the afternoon's triumphs.

"How did you come up with the Attic?" Marcellus asks.

"Fuck if I know," Gay Don says.

"And can you believe *this* character?" Robot says, arm around Nikki. "Pro-*seed*-cake? That was, seriously, a stroke of genius."

Marcellus agrees. "You pick something one iota less weird and we were gonna get stomped."

"First rule of performance art," Gay Don says. "It can never be bullshitty enough."

"I dunno," Nikki says. "You can only fuck with people so long, you know?"

"Wrong," Robot says. "You can fuck with them forever."

They get back in the Camry and drive home.

DUFF CALLS FROM REHAB, apologizes. His teeth practically gleam over the phone. Huge surprise, he met a guy in group, a drummer who played with the Ainsley Lord Experience. Who played with Screaming Jim Slim. Duff and the drummer lift together three days a week, cardio on Saturdays. Trust exercises. Buy each other shots of wheatgrass, carry tractor tires up hills. Duff says they're starting a new thing, "Super commercial, but hip, you know?"

"Not really."

Duff says that Nikki has to move to Brooklyn. Has to bring his killer bass tone. "The plan is to slay New York first, then hit Japan, and eventually own all of music itself."

There are whiffs of steps 4 through 7. There is the unmistakable resonance of true belief.

Tara listens to Nikki's half of the conversation, rolls her eyes. Tara leans over his back, says, *No way.* Tara says, *Thanks for nada.* Tara says, *Don't let him do this to you again.*

Nikki says thanks for nada.

"Wait, for real?" Duff says, preclick.

"I'm so proud of you," Tara says, pulls Nikki onto the bed. Later they go to Blockbuster and rent *Juno*, split a bottle of cabernet, open a second one but leave it on the counter.

Eight months later Nikki sees Duff windmilling power chords next to Paul Shaffer, getting the band nod from Letterman.

Give it up, ladies and gentlemen, for the Torrentials!

NIKKI CALLS A LAWYER, who laughs. Thirty days later he wakes up thirty.

Three decades old.

Might as well be ten.

He hits the occasional open mic, doesn't mind playing for beer, likes the feeling of a 90-watt spot on his face while a half-drunk softball team talks through the changes.

His best song is called "Rime of the Ancient Silas Marner."

No one laughs.

There is some disappointment.

But no regrets, because he's never going to be as good as the tool from the Strokes, let alone Charlie Parker, so why keep pretending?

Tara says he never wants to do anything fun.

Tara says he's getting fat.

Tara splits after a long talk conducted on two sleeping bags zippered together.

She takes the Cabriolet, leaves Rose.

Nikki holds out as long as he can, another couple winters, finally pawns the Thinline for next to nothing. Sells his amps and speakers and heads and pedals and straps and cords and tuners for even less. He donates the sax to an elementary school. All that's left is the acoustic, which he plays for his three-year-old daughter, who loves to dampen the buzzing strings with her tiny palm.

Rose especially digs Sly's "Family Affair," doesn't seem to mind that Nikki always fucks up the changes to "Good-bye Mr. Porkpie Hat."

"Daddy?"

"Yes?"

"Daddy?"

"Yes?"

Rose likes to start a question but never knows how to finish. For a second Nikki thinks that's a pretty good metaphor for every string he's ever plucked, every melody he's never written.

But then decides that's just more arty bullshit.

"Daddy?"

"Yes?"

Her little mouth trembles, desperate to force out something of value. Nikki can already tell by the time she's thirteen she'll cut her hair at an angle across her jaw, dye the tips purple, get a nose ring. She'll have posters of bands that don't exist yet above her bed and a leather-pant boyfriend. She'll crash a car and burn down a bodega and spend freshman year teaching herself to play Siouxsie on the trombone.

She's got the time, she's got the genes.

She's got the jones.

Nikki tries not to be jealous, fails.

"C'mere little petal," he says, plays Rose another song.

The Rescues

1995 Ford TraumaHawk SL Ambulance

The Dayton State Cornholers. Actually Musketeers, but still. They really only took Danny because of his willingness to hit. And be hit. His high school had made an unlikely run at the state lacrosse championship and it was more or less concluded his coarse and speeding bulk was the reason. There was a scholarship offer. He was thinking enlist. Strap on the Kevlar, get seriously ballistic. Also, he hated to study.

But the old man told him to smarten up.

"Have fun in Ohio. Try not to be a pussy."

By the second day Danny had a reputation. Bigger players stepped out of the way as he came tearing across the field, pads slapping, bent low for maximum collision.

"Chillax, brohman," they said, mimed doobie fingers. "It's only practice."

"Chillax this," he said, hit even harder.

There was a purity to mayhem. To split lips and sprung hamstrings, when mud tasted as good as blood. Coach started calling Danny "Junkyard." Girls stared in the caf. He became a minor god of chaos and cracked ribs, the terrifying silence of a blindside tackle or unattended erection. Danny's teammates jumped at the bite of his voice, soaked in the wisdom of his elbows, Saturday nights with pitchers of Bud and gathered blondes hazed with smoke and stories, *Then Junkyard flies over and absolutely destroys the dude! I bet he still hasn't gotten up!*

He took every dare. Eat a worm, run through traffic naked, follow that hulking waitress into a stall and make like a two-backed animal, moan loud enough for the entire bar to hear, release untold tiny flagellates across her skirt more than a little on purpose, leave proof of the negation of life itself.

Release being just another form of destruction.

Or, hey, maybe that's thinking too much. Fucking's fine but lacrosse is decisive. Put the ball in the net, tally it up. Put your man on his ass. Constantly. Assert a hominid dominance. Not out on the street after six tequilas and a trip to the drunk tank: within a grid and according to strict and unwavering rules. Because to face a rival in pads whose chest is made for nothing so much as to be stepped on, and then to do so, is a work of art that not only resists the censure of those who absorb no pain, who form opinions on the sidelines, but often results in the ability to sit in a packed bar all night long without a dollar in your pocket and howl for pitcher after pitcher of cheap beer utterly secure in the knowledge that someone will eventually bring it.

Junk-yard! Junk-yard! Junk-yard!

The third game of the season Danny took a cheap shot in the crease, bled out like a pig. Time was called. His teammates kicked at the dirt and swore revenge, without the sac to actually follow through. So he sat for forty-eight stitches with a fish hook and no anesthetic, sprinted from the locker room and doled near-Balkan retribution. The Cornholers won by eleven. Even Coach was like, "Bring it down a notch, Danny, they're gripping their pearls." And it was true, the other team full of guys with something better on the side, prelaw, premed, all of them suddenly asking, *Who needs this madness?*

Danny did.

Every second, minute, inch, foot.

Sweat and uniform and pads and stick.

The Cornholers rose in the standings, playoffs in sight for the first time in decades. Then the last game of the season a big-name Ivy League team rolled in, none of their players much except the midfielder, all jaw and shaved head. A towering Cossack with three-day stubble and yellow breath. His eyes were empty, lips flecked with blood.

"I've heard of you," the Cossack said.

"No you haven't."

"I've seen you play."

"No you didn't."

They danced and hacked and elbowed all the way across the field.

It hurt.

Danny watched as the Cossack clotheslined their forwards, dished cheap shots to the fullbacks, delivered pain with pro efficiency. With a radiant grin. There was no hesitation, no nuance. It was almost like being in the backyard with Dad again, running drills, pushing limits. Exploring the fine line between Just Doing It and puking a streak of Gatorade across the neighbor's fence.

"You and me? We could be friends," the Cossack whispered, as they chopped and muscled in front of goal. "Let's hang out, go to dinner and a show."

Danny knew he had to quip back. Be funny and casual. Arch and bold. But his shit talk was gone. The Clint stare, the Bruce smirk. He wanted to take off his spikes, feel his toes in the grass. He wanted to eat graham crackers dunked in milk, go home and lie under a quilt, watch something old and dumb like *Melrose Place*, the episode where Heather Locklear wears tight pants.

During timeouts the guys punched Danny's arm and shouted encouragements, confused by the loss of their beautiful madman.

Smack him! Shut his mouth, Junk!

Even coach wadded an entire pack of Dentyne.

Christ on a stick, Danny, you waiting for an invite?

In the third quarter he stole a pass and raced up the left sideline. A breakaway. Just the net and thirty open yards. The goalie waited, resigned. They both knew Danny was going to score and then pretend like he couldn't control his momentum, feed the dude sixty pounds of marinated shoulder.

There was no sound, no sweat, no grass.

Just his feet, just his breath.

And then the Cossack coming.

Fast and from behind.

A low giggle, the heavy tromp of cleat.

They connected with a slobber-crack that echoed across the field, rose through the stands, halted the game.

An hour later Danny woke in the ambulance while a nurse with a Kid 'n Play lid hooked him to a tube. It felt like he was wearing himself sideways.

"Did we win?"

"I doubt it."

"There a problem?"

The nurse slipped Danny her phone number. "After the surgery? You decide you don't need them leftover Oxys, you give me a call."

That night the entire squad gathered around the bed, stared at his leg in traction, the pins in his hip, said all the things you say, relieved when the orderly finally kicked them out.

The article in the campus paper was intentionally vague, combed by a paralegal for liability.

A week went by, then three, then six.

Six teammates visited, then three, then none.

Some pimply kid cleaned out Danny's locker, dropped off his gear jammed into two Ninja Turtles pillowcases. He was allowed to stay enrolled, but no more scholarship. "The good news is you can concentrate on your classes," a counselor of some sort suggested. Friends stared at their onion rings while Danny limped through the caf. He'd pass the team on the quad, all the chillaxers and brohmen lowering their eyes, his torn gait evidence of something damning.

Maybe even contagious.

Transformation was, according to a textbook he'd partially read, inevitable.

The walker became crutches became a cane.

He dropped out, put on weight.

"Oh, wow," people said in the produce aisle, at the movies. "You still in town?"

Danny found the ambulance chick's number, called her up. The next day he got a job delivering pizza, put a deposit on an apartment off campus, right above a comic book shop. The owner tended to frown while he limped though the stacks, showed off his scars, winked at nerdy girls, lifted a few Green Lanterns.

Is the Fist of Power lost forever?!!? the covers asked. *Will a monarch emerge from within the Demon Chrysalis?!!?*

1983 Plymouth Scamp "Pizza Monster" Delivery Truck

It was nearly midnight on a rush order, window down, radio blaring. The classics. Verse, chorus, verse. *Buh-buh-buh Bennie and the Jets.* The DJ complained about the heat. The stink of pepperoni rose from the floorboards. Zeppelin was next, with their grunts and squeals, their Middle Earth routine. It was like, if the dude was such a Druid, why was he trying so hard to sound black?

Danny spotted a glint of chrome on the side of the road, locked 'em up. In a clearing stood an ultimate Frisbee squad, coed, mud-flecked, ponytails and orange slices. Their van steamed, hood propped with a Wiffle bat. He wanted to give them all a hug for thinking that ironic things had actual meaning, their discounted sneakers and sailor tattoos and patchy facial hair.

"Y'all need some help?"

They cheered.

He eased out of the cab, limped across the double yellows.

The cheering stopped.

"Holy shit," someone said.

Danny tended to forget he was him. Broken. Looming. Might as well rock a leather apron and a chainsaw.

A girl in hot pants stepped forward, aimed something shiny and black.

"Shoot," he said.

Her lighter illuminated the engine, a knot of rust and

ticking heat. Danny leaned over and pretended to tighten a hose, spelled out his name in crankcase grease.

"Okay, fire it up."

Hot Pants slid behind the wheel and jammed in the key. The van magically roared to life, air thick with ozone and the tang of high fives.

"Oh, fuck it," Hot Pants said, and jumped into Danny's arms.

Everyone laughed. Beers were retrieved from the cooler, the radio cranked. Bros danced with bros, whitely and without shame. Danny stood in the middle of it all, drinking in just the sort of love that can only come from an ultimate Frisbee team on the side of the road in the cricket-heavy dark.

2009 Black Acura "Sport Package" ZDX

By August he was resurrecting two cars a week. Sorority girls and math department heads. Adjuncts and transfers. The occasional rumpled provost. It was a small college town, dark country roads, way too easy to get stuck or stranded.

Word got back to Pizza Monster.

Mikey Atta spun dough on his middle finger, dared Danny to charge fifty a car. Hippie Tim buttoned his tweed jacket, said it was a lawsuit on a platter. Gail, sweaty-pink and nearly poured into her waitress uniform, said everyone had one important skill in life and Danny's was to rescue people.

"You're an automotive Saint Bernard."

Mikey Atta leaned through the pass and air-wristed a blow job. The busboys fell out in hysterics. A woman looking at the menu frowned, took her son by the elbow, let the screen door slam.

"So what's your one important skill?" Danny asked.

"Folding napkins," Gail said, finishing another pile. She had short bangs and cat eye glasses, spoke out of the corner of her mouth in a sardonic way that waitresses with advanced degrees now living off campus with a guy named Zach sometimes tended to. It was no secret that Danny wanted to spend entire shifts carnally entwined, locked in the walk-in while Gail's hot breath and cries for mercy defrosted several flats of ricotta. It was also no secret to her boyfriend, Zach, who didn't like it a bit, but got one look at Danny's enormous shaved head and swollen knuckles and decided to be evolved about the whole thing.

"You got something for me?" she whispered.

Danny took the cash and slipped a baggie into her apron pocket.

"Incoming!" Hippie Tim yelled. It was his one important skill: radar. Ten seconds later a booth's worth of sorority girls gaggled in, ordered a round of side salads, and then went to town on free breadsticks.

Mikey Atta flicked his tongue between two fingers.

Tom Petty oozed from the juke.

Danny stood out on the deck, where a black Acura circled the lot, laid a patch all the way down the street.

"Delivery up!" Hippie Tim yelled, sliding round glasses back up his nose. "You think you can you handle this one, Danny, or should I call in the National Guard?"

1969 Porsche 911 T

Bob Devine had been ordering an X-large with sausage and peppers three nights a week since his wife emptied the closets and took the twins to her mother's in Corfu. She left a note peanut-buttered to the wall letting Professor Devine know where he could stick his teaching assistant, a fey Asian kid with Elvis sideburns. Three months later Elvis transferred to Duke, leaving behind a suitcase full of uncorrected papers and a formal harassment complaint now working its way through dual ethics panels. The only thing the professor got to keep was the mortgage and an ancient Porsche up on blocks, extradition hopeless, the twins destined to hit puberty under the cruel Ionian sun.

He opened the door before Danny could even knock. Boxers, chest hair, silk robe. They'd had one class, History of Some Shit or Another. Danny was still on scholarship then. Cocky and entitled. Pawing at girls. Never did the reading, never knew the answers. Shiloh. Yalta. Teapot Dome.

Professor Devine lifted the lid, grabbed a slice, shoved it deep.

"Is America wonderful or what?"

"As long as you're American."

"Well, all empires have their flaws. But few have unlimited toppings."

"Or unlimited credit."

Devine added two quarters to the bill, unaware that SHITTY TIPPER blinked on the screen every time he ordered. Gail, whose one important skill was actually coding Linux, set the system up. SHITTY TIPPER was license for Mikey Atta to loogie the mozz, to crimp the professor's dough with a grease-black sneaker print before ladling sauce. At first Danny was against it, but was now fairly sure it made no difference. Every single thing in every single restaurant in the world has been on the floor at least once.

"Hey, you wouldn't happen to have any extra *napkins*, would you?"

"How many you need?"

Professor Devine held up sixty dollars.

Danny took it, palmed over a baggie.

"Don't eat the whole thing at once."

Professor Devine smiled.

"I have no idea how you ever failed my class."

1993 Nissan Pulsar NX

A mile down the road a car was pulled over, hazards on. A girl stood embossed in brake light. Tall, Persian, smirking. Born to ruin teachers and preachers, mock family values on yards of thigh alone. Or maybe just really pretty.

"Need a hand?"

"Nice hat."

Danny turned the purple cap around. Nothing to be done about the rest of the uniform, khakis and a polo shirt. Even the truck was purple, a graphic of Frankenstein on the hood going, "Grrr . . . Me no skimp on toppings!"

He rolled out jumper cables, tried not to limp.

"Hey, I recognize you."

"*Texas Chainsaw*? That was someone else."

The girl laughed. "No, I used to come to games. Up in the bleachers, a bunch of us with a jug of wine."

"Cheering away?"

"Depended on the score."

Danny clamped the batteries together, as always expecting a sudden jolt to fuse his teeth. Instead, the Nissan roared to life. Flowers swayed in the halogens. The radio kicked in, a dissonant trombone blaring out of speakers more expensive than the rest of the car put together.

"Who's this?"

She cranked the knob, drowning out frogs and grasshoppers nestled in the weeds.

"Sun Ra."

They faced each other, covered with sweat. Haze hung like a wet sheet above the oily grass and between the oaks.

"What's your name?"

"Steak."

Danny knew it was a test. If he made a dumb joke, like *medium rare* or *well done* or *free range*, she'd immediately cross him off the list, the same method she'd erased four years' worth of frat boys with.

"Hey, Steak?"

"What?"

"Wanna go out sometime?"

She smiled, hair impossibly long and Nile black, swung it out of her face like a flag of victory. "We're already out."

Danny watched as she folded herself back into the car, spun the wheel, fishtailed away.

2004 Volkswagen Vanagon

He found her in an old student directory. Stalled for an hour then dialed. No answer. Redialed. Voicemail. Danny left a message while Hippie Tim wrote him up for making calls on company time. In the kitchen, Mikey Atta snapped a towel at the ass of the busboy who wore a turban. A girl at the counter who'd been gazing at the menu like it was the New Testament finally asked if the Spinach Goddess came with extra spinach.

"Cold pies getting colder!" Hippie Tim yelled, rang the bell.

Danny gunned it across town. First a raft of sausage subs to the bio lab, along with two baggies of Vicodin. Then a departmental meeting, twelve wilted salads and a smaller baggie for the security guard, a dude named Heavy Kev, who let Danny in even on nights it was obvious he was fronting an empty box.

On the way back his phone buzzed.

Steak, Steak, Steak.

"Danny?" a secretary said. "Hold for your father."

Fuck, fuck, fuck.

"You there?"

"Sort of."

"Any news about the team?"

"No."

"What about coaching?"

"What about it?"

"My office has a few open slots. You buy a tie, I could place you."

"I already have a job."

"Bussing crusts?"

"There's profit in humility."

"Christ, even your voice is fat. You sound like I should send you a bra."

"Actually, what you should send me is three thousand dollars."

His father slipped out of permanent hard-on mode.

"Are you serious?"

Danny was.

The ambulance chick who wrapped his knee, name of Miss Kay, bought his entire script of Oxy after all. He'd decided to tough it out, ignore the pain. Needed the cash. When those were gone, they met for a beer, talked through shopping doctors, what to say, how to beg without begging. Danny came up with a few flourishes, thought with some practice he might even bust out tears on command. She nodded. "Big dude with a cringe? Puppy eyes like you got? Shit, I'd write you for three refills myself."

When the clinic finally cut him off, a male nurse with a nose ring sent out front to say next time it was the cops on speed dial, Miss Kay offered Danny a job.

"On the ambulance?"

"No, in the saddle."

"Wait, what?"

"Pill donkey. You apply somewhere does take-out. Thai, Chinese, whatever. Keep your tips, make special deliveries for me on the side."

Hippie Tim hired Danny the next day.

Within a month he started to skim. Shorted baggies, palmed aspirin for Oxy, pocketed the difference. It was really dumb. Like Miss Kay was never gonna find out. Like numerous painfully unhigh adjuncts wouldn't demand refunds. Like whole dorms full of underopiated sophomores would fail to vow revenge.

"Dad, I'm in real trouble here."

"You spent three large on a girl?"

"No, a tattoo."

"You gotta be shitting me."

Danny wasn't. It was pure old-school, Yakuza-style, from thigh to clavicle, carp and koi and an intricate blood-red moon slung over rows of Japanese waves. Twenty-six hours of table time already, on his stomach, an orgy of pain as an ancient woman with a bamboo stick jabbed ribbons of black and orange beneath his every surface and delicate layer.

"Give Mom a kiss," Danny said, hanging up as a black Acura pulled from the 7-Eleven with a screech. Windshield smoked, chrome grill, shiny and mean. It cut off four cars and got right on his bumper.

Danny switched lanes.

The Acura switched lanes.

He switched again.

The Acura switched again.

Dad rang, went to voicemail.

Delivery texts poured in. Hippie Tim.

RUSH ORDER.

PEPPERONI.

DICK HEAD.

Danny played it cool, smoothed across campus like, *hey, no problem*, and then at the six-way stop by the bowling alley punched it way late through a red. There was a chorus of horns as he swept under the entrance to the state park. The little truck howled, blew by picnic tables and families and statues of founding Whigs, a purple blur through the high rolling switchbacks until he was absolutely sure there was nothing behind him except an old couple in a Vanagon taking pictures through their windshield.

1961 Ford Fairlane Taxi

"Where to?"

Danny repeated the address, chewing his tongue to ribbons. For some reason he'd dry-swallowed four Adderall from the case Miss Kay bought off a guy named Taco she met at Pilates. The pills jumped all over him right away, a thousand cups of coffee with a 120-volt chaser. His head felt light and untethered, like it might just float up out the window and through the atmosphere, begin taking cloud samples.

"You sure this is the place?" the driver asked, idling in front of vaguely Soviet concrete apartments. A pack of kids taunted each other crunching gravel circles on their ten-speeds. They gave Danny the finger, whirled off down the street.

"Yeah, this is it."

Steak opened the door wearing a faded dress, straight from the Kansas Tornado collection, barefoot, beautiful.

Also, all her hair was gone.

Every inch, head gleaming, scalp shorn white. Her eyes dared Danny to be shocked, another test.

"Something's different," he said. "New perfume?"

She smiled and walked into the kitchen.

"You hungry?"

He wasn't. Jangly-high, zero appetite.

"Starving."

They chopped side by side, boiled water, made sauce from scratch, those goofy little cans of tomato paste that seem to contain nothing at all. When the penne was ready Danny rinsed it, a couple going over the edge. They lay in the sink, pale and soft, abandoned.

"We lost a few good men today."

Steak laughed.

"Want to hear a story?"

"Sure."

It was about this meathead campus hero, let's call him Donny, and the feats of madness and stupidity she personally witnessed him perform back in the day. Like the time Donny rode a bike in the library naked, or the time he spray-painted JESUS SAVES SOULS AND RECLAIMS THEM FOR VALUABLE CASH PRIZES across the face of the student union, or the time he put an M-80 in a bucket of ranch dressing in the caf. How funny it all was. How tough and raw and compelling he had been. How, despite the fratishness and cult of moronicism it seemed to engender—just the sort of thing she normally despised—how inexplicably hot Donny had made her.

"Yeah, whatever happened to that guy?"

She got up and walked into the bedroom, kicked dirty towels into a closet. He lined up Adderall like a parade, crushed their dreams with the back of a spoon. They banged rails, compounds breaking down, binding together, a slurry of toxic waste seeping into all the appropriate organs.

"This is good. This is just what I needed," she said, a trickle of blood from one nostril.

"This is bad. This is not what you need," he said, wiping it away.

Steak pulled off her dress. Her breasts lolled in opposite directions.

"Jesus."

"Hera," she said, knelt and began to lick the tissue around his ruined knee, trace the raw crossing lines. The scars rose, a livid white and then pink, her fingernails following the waves of his tattoo, around the sun and sky and schools of hungry koi.

For an album side they worked their way across the length and width of her futon. It was sensory immersion, action without thought, armpit and convexity and gentle undulation. There was no goal, nothing to attain. At intervals throughout the night she got up for smokes or to change the music. Danny got up to soap his stinking neck and fish out another baggie. Dawn came. They sweated through noon, drank more wine, ordered food. She licked his asshole. He bit her thigh. It was dinner and then midnight and then in a granular, panting lull they listened to Mingus, which Danny knew because Steak said "This is Charles Mingus." The music was a carnival orchestra, like being jabbed with a fork. It whirled and beeped and honked with glee. In the center of the bedlam was Charlie, who held it all together, plucked away at his bass, sang and hummed and drove the other musicians like sled dogs across the tundra. At any other time Danny would likely have hated this prophet, this Charles Mingus. He would have snapped the dial, searched for ZZ Top or "Separate Ways," but now, lying across Steak, he understood. Genius was a code pulsed down from a binary star, a revelatory percussive wave. It was math plus rhythm, an equation of intervals, the sound and then not the sound, something that could never be snorted or faked or even approached by the fastest, most devastating sprint across an open, grassy field.

HE WOKE FROM a dream about transmission schematics. Mostly for German sports cars of various makes and vintages, but mainly the 1957 DKW Monza, when Steak kicked the mattress.

She was showered, head powdered, wearing a clean dress.

"It's Monday."

"So?"

She gave him a glass of ice water and stroked his forehead, on the verge of confiding something. Even from the depths of his hangover, the cracked porcelain of his brainpan, Danny knew it was too soon for a declaration of love.

But he was wrong.

Steak told him that she was truly, deeply in love.

With her girlfriend.

The one out of town on a roofing job.

Who was coming home.

Soon.

He rolled over and the room rolled with him. "A make-popcorn-while-watching-lawyer-shows-in-pajamas-together kind of girlfriend?"

"No."

The girlfriend's name was Lula. Lula worked as a carpenter. Lula had broad shoulders and thick, callused hands that felt like loving bark on Steak's soft and spoken-for hips.

Also, she was very sorry.

Steak confessed to being empathic, which would make for a bad cable television series but was still a rare and inexplicable gift. She explained that Danny was one of those people with a strain of need running so deeply through their core that she had no defense against it. Steak said this sort of person, him, sometimes barged into her life and ruined everything stable she'd worked so hard to build. She said Danny was a destroyer. A barbarian at the gate. Both emotionally and sexually. Physically and mentally. And right this moment, on an early Monday morning, she had briefly managed to wrest back control.

"So, can you please leave? Like, now?"

He stood, naked, covered in the patchy sheen of their commingling. The bodily proof of forty-eight hours of a deep and genuine connection.

"You're shitting me, right?"

Steak scratched her calf with the other foot, balanced on one leg like the rare tidal bird she was. If the look on her face signaled anything, it was pure dismay.

And possibly the desire for fresh shellfish.

That Car Again

Danny got to Pizza Monster four hours late, the lot mostly empty.

Except for a mean-looking black Acura, all rims and grill.

His stash was in the walk-in. His cash was in his locker.

For a second Danny considered turning around and driving the truck west, keep going until he ran out of gas or maps.

A guy with a bulge in his waistband sat at the counter. He had huge hands and a nylon jacket and looked like an extra from a movie about swindling the London mob. Danny was scared, but probably not as much as he should be. If the life of a student was one long bong hit leavened with intermittent study, the life of an adult was the acknowledgment that there was only one rule: Everyone gets what they deserve.

Gail was talking to Hippie Tim by the salad bar. Mikey Atta's forearms shed flour as he snapped a rolled-up towel at the ass of the busboy with the strawberry birthmark. Danny slid next to Miss Kay in the upholstered corner booth.

Her Afro stood straight up, like a silo. She wore blue eye shadow, pretty like a Jackie O blazer: trim, immaculate, lost to another era.

"You're late."

"Yeah."

"Bossman says you're a shitty worker."

"Hard to argue there."

"How's the knee?"

"Gone. Thrashed."

Miss Kay tapped salt on her wrist and licked it.

"So in terms of problems that matter, you got my money?"

"No."

"You got my drugs?"

"Mostly no."

The big guy at the counter swung around. Danny turned over a fork, readied the tines.

"Look, I know I messed up, but is this necessary?"

"Come again?"

The guy yanked at the bulge in his waistband. Gail walked over to the register. He aimed his wallet, paid, left a nice tip. A station wagon with a bunch of screaming kids idled into the lot. The guy got in the passenger seat and kissed the woman driving. They looked both ways before pulling back into traffic.

"Wait, he's not yours?"

"Mine?"

"The muscle," Danny said. "Tailing me around town."

Air passed between Miss Kay's lips, more dismissive than angry. "You donkey. I'm not having anyone follow you."

"You telling me that's not your Acura?"

They both looked out the window. The Acura wasn't there anymore. In its spot was a Fiat. And next to that was a silver Hyundai with the license plate NURSE1.

"You wanna live on my salary, you're welcome to try. But this isn't the movies. You think I'd work with your dumb ass if I could afford muscle?"

Danny considered the possibility that he was deeply immature.

"Probably no."

"Probably no," Miss Kay agreed.

The Hobart clonked through a rinse cycle. The jukebox blared, Axl warbling about the relative sweetness o' his child. When he was done, Bob Seger turned the page.

"Now do me a favor, genius, and go see if my pizza is ready."

1965 Cadillac Convertible

Eventually fall dropped in full, red and black, orange leaves sweeping though the grass like arson. Danny put on an extra shirt, changed the antifreeze in the truck. Then Gail announced she was pregnant and quit. A day later Gail's boyfriend, Zach, came looking for Mikey Atta with a claw hammer, and Mikey Atta quit, too. The busboy with the turban, name of Sandip, now manned the ovens. He was a wizard with crust. Business picked up. Hippie Tim tied on an apron and started waiting tables himself. Business dropped off again.

Danny cranked the radio, waited for texts, cruised the school grounds in ever-widening circles. Past dorms and clinics, past the field house and lacrosse pitch, past groups of kids running shuttles or down on one knee, crosses dug into the grass like spears as they absorbed strategy and tactics, ready to kill each other for the slightest nod of affirmation.

He swept through the gates and the guard booths, back over the interstate, where the strip malls ended and the bargain stores began. Wings and burgers and even faster foods. Smoothies and yoga studios. The bar next to the other bar.

Just beyond a litter-strewn turnaround was a glint of chrome.

Danny locked 'em up, reversed the length of a football field, and pulled alongside a powder-blue, magnificently finned Cadillac stalled in the weeds.

Al Rubirosa, short for Álvaro, had failed Danny in sculpture. Hard to blame him, since Danny hardly ever showed up for class and even when he did knocked out dumb things like cock-bongs, the kind of things that would make a professor hate you. But Danny loved the way the professor seemed unsurprised to find him clomping toward the vintage Caddy. How he didn't act like it was anything worth mentioning that Danny pushed him and his family into the BoxxMart lot and tried a jump, which failed, his whole affect more or less saying, *I need help and you are providing it. Such is a transaction among honorable men.*

The professor's wife, Galena, walked to the store while they leaned under the hood, pointed at this wire or that valve and conjectured as to each one's purpose or possible blame. She soon returned with bags of food. They laid out a blanket between two minivans for a picnic. Their little boy and two girls laughed and squealed and jumped in Danny's lap, calling him el Cucuy. Danny didn't ask what it meant and they didn't say. A bottle of wine was opened. Then a second. It began to drizzle, but they pretended not to notice. Galena had a chipped tooth and freckled clavicles. She smoked and laughed at Danny's jokes, which the professor did not, but in a way that seemed simply a matter of taste instead of a judgment.

"And why is it," she asked, "you are such the terrible student?"

Danny told her.

School, knee, pizza, Steak.

Drugs, donkey, Miss Kay's wage-garnishment plan.

The Rubirosas nodded, grunted, poured more wine.

They ate baguettes with ham and mayonnaise.

Galena finally suggested that all lives are messy, as are all loves. She referenced D. H. Lawrence, as well as H. L. Mencken. Álvaro described the exquisite flaws of Giacometti the Younger, the long and beautiful curves of Jean Arp.

They encouraged him to re-enroll, take more classes.

They encouraged him to cease his criminal behavior.

They encouraged him to call Steak, profess his love.

"You must settle things with this woman, or you will stagnate."

"Yes," Álvaro said. "To pine for someone without return is the worst of all afflictions."

Danny dialed, hit speakerphone.

Lula answered. She described a standpipe that had given her trouble all day, talked about the difficulty of hiring laborers in winter. Danny told her about bad tippers and the price of gas. Finally, Lula wished him well. She also wished he wouldn't call anymore.

"Like, ever. You know what I'm saying here, Danny?"

He did.

"So perhaps it was not to be," Galena concluded, with a shrug that encompassed the folly of believing in salvation, but particularly as delivered at the foot of a woman.

"Yes," Álvaro said, swirled his wine.

Eventually the tow truck came and a hard little man yanked the Caddy up onto his winch.

For once Danny was no help at all.

Al and Galena piled the kids into the backseat of the tow like the whole thing was a grand adventure. Danny kissed them all good-bye, especially the shy, brown-kneed daughters with their charming mispronunciation of Daniel, with their stoic knowledge of exactly who he was and how they would avoid his ilk when the time or puberty came, but for now cheek-to-cheek in the established continental style.

They waved and sang and were gone.

Danny's phone buzzed.

It was a text, wrong number, five words.

IT'S A NEW DAY, BAE.

He decided that wisdom, if it ever came, would always be beamed down from above.

Without explanation or warning.

A pulse from a just God.

Or just god.

Maybe even a genial satellite.

He fired up the engine, mashed the gas, merged without signalling.

Prepared to go forth and deliver.

Hey Monkey Chow

Jonelle's pregnant, huge in a red one-piece, pissed because Cher came, too. In a bikini. Half of Ocean Beach staring. Also because there's a dirt bike and packs of dogs. Because there's a too-loud radio and abandoned food and herds of teenagers smoking cigarettes, one after another.

Someone yells, "Shark!" The lifeguard yawns. A little girl runs by with a Popsicle in her mouth. Her lips are blue.

"It's dirty here," Jonelle says.

"It's called sand," Cher says.

One of the teenagers walks over. He's wearing a necklace. "You Dillard?"

"Maybe."

"You gotta go see Butterfly."

I had no idea he was back in town. Or even alive.

"Who says?"

"The man do."

A dog races in from the water, shakes itself off. Jonelle yelps, turns, presses her torpedo stomach into mine. The only thing to do is kiss her so much she can't see straight.

"Stop, you'll hurt the baby."

"It's okay, we'll make another one."

"So not funny," Jonelle says, but lets me dry her legs. "And who in fuck is Butterfly?"

THE DAY BEFORE CHRISTMAS in fourth grade Wade's mom won a monkey in a card game, a scabby little thing in a wire cage, crazy eyes and a permanent hard-on. It shit every twelve seconds. We heard it screech all night long. The next morning the monkey was on its side, wouldn't move. Wade figured it was either dead or hungry, slid the gate banana-wide. The thing elbowed through, sank its choppers into Wade's nose, wouldn't let go until the old lady in 6A shot it with a pistol so rusty it crumbled in her hand. At the clinic they made a graft, took eight inches of butt skin to close the hole, stitches and a pink butterfly in the center of Wade's face, an ass-papillon, hard to look at, hard not to look at.

After that Mom was all, "Why don't you go play with Wade?" Cher winked like, *Because, um, yuk?* and I poked her under the table like, *Do I have to?* and then Mom gave me the stare, rubbing her stomach like, *How did something so stupid ever find its way out?*

"Okay, fine."

I walked down the hall. Wade's mom cracked the door in a nightie. Skinny and bruised, pubic hair a mystery half-solved beneath shiny cotton.

"Yeah?"

"Butterfly around?"

She rested her hand on the front of my corduroys. "You're a good kid."

So me and Cher would hang with Wade on the front stoop, play Hold'em for dimes or Skittles until the bus came. *You beat a king-high straight? Fuck, no. You beat trip sixes? Fuck, no.* Wade liked to squeeze Cher's wrist, *Don't let her deal, she cheats!* I'd warn him to cut the shit and Cher would be like, *I don't need no protection*, and sweep up all the dimes.

Older dudes on the stroll would check us out, laugh some, but never say much, like Wade was so messed up it wasn't even worth it.

School was different. Before class, after class, recess. *Hey, Monkey Chow!* and *Only the nose knows!* and *How'm I suppose to eat lunch if he don't turn and face the wall?* Wade kept getting infected. Walked around with a special bag of swabs and creams, constantly punched in the neck and behind the swings. He needed another graft. He needed a more sterile environment. The principal finally dialed up Stu Mayse, who'd been caught fondling twins but then found Jesus and opened Amayzing Grace and Grocery, mostly giving back to the community in the form of double coupons but in this case told he was funding a scholarship or else. Stu Mayse ponied the cash. There was a cut ribbon and flashbulbs in front of the register, a feel-good story that everyone would feel a whole lot better about once Wade was out of town. They handed him a train ticket and a Samsonite, a new hat and sweater, sent to a school for specials all the way down in Santa Monica, gone nearly eight years.

I SKIP BREAKFAST, tell Jonelle I've got the morning shift.

"But you don't open until noon."

Her stomach pushes out of pajama tops, beautiful and exhausted, sweaty and pissed, all thigh and frown. I explain how two taps are busted, which is true, and that I gotta get there early to flush the lines, which isn't, Manny on his stool at the end of the bar like, "Assholes wanna drink that perfumy shit, they can do it out of bottles."

I wait at the bus stop until I'm sure Jonelle's not peeking behind the curtain and then practically jog over to Seventy-Seventh, wanting to get it over with. The building's in the middle of a block of pitted brick and layered tags, Wade's apartment on the top floor. No elevator. Stairs dark and long and falling apart. I knock and there are like six locks, flip, flip, flip, a bar and a latch and a bolt and a guy, tall and cut, closing it all behind me.

"Um, Butterfly?"

He points. "Yeah, but the man don't like that name no more."

There are empty rooms. A TV, a table, half a rug. A chew

toy chewed to shit. Wade sits at a desk in back, folding up powder, glossy little triangles piled next to a cell phone that rings, rings.

"Hey, Dillard," he says, and it's amazing, the difference. The kid with the suitcase and sweater got left behind. Now Wade's bigger than the desk, all shoulders and arms. The scar has changed, too, like borders redrawn after long negotiations, the graft and his face having come to terms on the subject of just how pink, just how awful. "Word is you're hitched."

"Have been a while now."

"Little wife, little house?"

"I guess."

"Your sister crashing with you?"

Cher's not really my sister. She's adopted. Or more like her mom left her on our couch with half a box of Pampers and never came back. My friends were always like, *Yo, Dilly, you ever watch your sister take a shower?* or *Yo, Dilly, you guys play special games down in the basement?* Mainly because Cher grew up tall and quick, with green assassin's eyes, with long red hair and long pale legs, long and smooth and freckled everything. I was always, *Dudes, we're practically related,* and they were always, *Practically is an invitation,* and I was like, *But still and shit* and they were like, *You gotta expand your horizons, player, even nuns do anal now.*

"Yeah, she is."

Wade laughs. "Do I love your game or what? Quiet Dilly. Goes along, gets along. Meanwhile it's Hef's place over there, Dilly pouring cognac, spinning Al Green."

The phone vibrates. He answers, says one word, hangs up.

"Tell you what, do me a solid and tell Cher to come by sometime."

"What for?"

"I wanna talk."

"Here?"

Butterfly puts his cowboy boots up on the desk, powder blue and tooled.

"Yeah, Dillard. Here."

I DON'T EVEN KNOW why Cher's home, a couple weeks ago just rolled in all, "Wait, for real? Your wife's name is *Jonelle*?"

"Well, yeah."

"She black?"

"She's from Connecticut."

"So?"

"Her parents are hippies. Her brother's name is like, Track. Or Twig."

"You don't remember?"

"It's a brain lock."

"A mental block?"

"Trunk, maybe? Trapper? We don't see them much. Or really at all."

"How come?"

"It's like a compound they live on. Gardens and a teepee. Compost piles."

"So where'd you and Jo-Jo meet?"

"She comes in, asks for this tropical drink."

"You still at Manny's?"

"Yeah."

"You make good tips?"

I look around the house like, *Bet your ass I do*, but it was the hippies who fronted the down payment.

Cher yanks my belt loop. "Guess what I really wanna know."

"Where to find a cheap place to stay?"

"No, dumbass. You miss your sister or what?"

I did. Just hanging out. Laughing at shit wasn't even funny. Wrestling on the plaid couch. The way she'd toss back her hair and roll the dice, slide the top hat on over to Ventnor Avenue.

"Yeah, not so much."

"At first I figured it was Jehovahs again," Jonelle says, easing down the stairs. "This voice I keep hearing but don't recognize."

They do the fake shake, the air kiss, compliment each other's shoes, laugh about being half-sisters now, all *Wow, your stomach's big*, and *Wow, you're older than I thought*, clasping hands and deciding, *Hey, maybe we should hit the mall together sometime, shop for cute onesies and a manicure*.

Then Jonelle pulls me aside, hair pulled back, one dangling streak of pink.

"No effing way she's staying with us."

"But we're family."

"Not even."

"Still."

Jonelle points to Mom's room, which would be the baby's but isn't. "You got any cousins we could move in, too?"

Actually I did—a rocker in Seattle running out of things to rhyme *heroin* with, and then one who deals blackjack up in Reno, would surf the couch faster than I could offer, ride it for life.

"No."

"Liar," Cher says from the other room.

I kiss Jonelle's shoulder, roll the waist of her sweatpants up and down, whisper *It's cool*, and *I got this*, palm the baby who kicks kicks kicks like he can barely wait.

She puts her mouth to my ear, "Who in fuck you think you're playing?"

And then heads to Parenting Now class.

The door slams, signal for Mom to come out of her room. She asks if anyone wants soup like Cher's been gone maybe half an hour. I point Mom in the right direction, get her tray ready, slippers ready, Bible near the pillow. All around the bed are candles and rosaries, pictures of men in uniforms and hats, unsmiling like there's something real important they have to do, if only it wasn't just out of frame.

Later, everyone's asleep and it's just me and Cher flipping channels, *sszzt, sszzt, sszzt*. There's car chases and pointy lawyers and shows where most people can't sing but some can and then everyone votes for the one that can't anyway. I find an old Archie Bunker, the episode where he's mad at Edith.

"She's got some ass on her," Cher says, wearing shorts and

socks and a T-shirt that says NO MEANS MAYBE in sparkly letters.

"Who, Jonelle?"

"No, Sally Struthers."

"What can I say? I like my shit thick."

Cher throws a pillow. Nails me in the face.

"Nailed you in the face."

"Hey, can I ask you something?"

"Nope."

"Like, what happened to college?"

"It wasn't college, okay Dilly? Why does everyone keep saying college?"

"What was it then?"

She sticks her nose in the air, arches her back. "Modeling school. Where you go to learn how to stand. And turn. And sniff."

"Sniff what?"

"Drugs. Skinny drugs. Pounds-off drugs."

"For real?"

"Not me, just some other girls."

"Did Terrence know?"

Cher laughs. Terrence being the one who spotted her on Ocean Beach. Gave her his card, which even Mom figured for horseshit, yeah right, he's scouting for *talent*. Two days later my boys boost a Nissan, pick me up. We pass a bottle all the way into the city, ready to kick Terrence's ass, bang bang bang on the door, and then fall into a lobby so white and clean, frozen air and brushed steel, like the set for a movie about futuristic haircuts. Terrence comes out, little mustache, deep swish. Harmless. Hands around flutes of champagne and crackers, introduces us to the same assistant twice. We leave the car with one tire up on the sidewalk, take the BART home. A month later photos arrive, glossy 8x10s that Mom shows to everyone not slinging dope or ass for half a mile, and even some of those. Terrence circulates his own, agencies and schools, gets Cher a full ride down in L.A., room and board and even study materials covered.

"So you didn't like it? I mean, Mom said she heard you liked it."

"Sure, why not?"

"Then how come you're back?"

"Oh, I dunno. I guess it's hard to go to class when you're pregnant."

I pick up the remote. Archie hits the turlet. Credits roll. Then a commercial for a Kawasaki that looks like a lunar lander. Maybe one day I'll get a bike, ride it all the way up to Oregon, drink some of that good coffee, cut a hard line through the switchbacks along Route 1, take dumb chances in and out of every bluff.

"You know what's weird, though? You don't really look pregnant."

Cher yawns.

"That's because I got *un*pregnant. Okay, Dilly?"

. . .

HER SUITCASE STAYS next to the sofa for a month, every night TV and pretzels and not much to say. Especially about her chapped lips and bouncy knee and the hickeys that ring her neck like pearls.

Jonelle refuses to leave the bedroom: *How much longer?* and *Isn't this our house?* and *Some people pay this thing called rent.* I bring up ice creams and sodas. I bring up magazines and kisses. Sometimes the magazines help, especially ones about the heiress who looks like a fish, or about Brad Pitt, who sleeps with this mannequin that adopted half of Equatorial New Guinea.

"What am I supposed to do, kick my own sister out?"

"Yes."

I lay my palm on Jonelle's stomach. "And what kind of example would that be setting for him or her?"

"Oh, please."

After dinner Cher has an announcement.

Mom's all, "What is it? Cancer?"

"I'm fine," Cher says.

"She's fine, Ma. It's okay."

"So you're going back? Are you going back to school?"

Cher grabs three fingers of hair, arranges it on top of her head.

"Actually, I'm getting married."

"To who?"

"Just a guy from the neighborhood," Cher says.

"See? A guy from the neighborhood, Ma. It's okay."

"Is it someone we know?"

"Definitely," Cher says.

WADE RENTS OUT the whole VFW and everyone just stands there, hot and sweaty in powder-blue suits, grumbling around the cash bar. Jonelle stays at home with Dilly Jr., new and perfect and healthy pink, so beautiful I can barely breathe, letting him exhale for both of us. Mom's not feeling so hot, can't make it either.

All the flowers say, COMPLIMENTS OF AMAYZING GRACE AND GROCERY!

All the Diet Cokes say, COMPLIMENTS OF AMAYZING GRACE AND GROCERY!

There are ten tables, ten couples, ten dudes who sling glossy triangles on ten corners.

Somehow I get through the dinner and the speeches, don't say a word. My collar's too tight, shoes too small, one beer follows another as Kool and the Gang *Cel-e-brate, good times, c'mon* while my sister and her train of lace spin across the floor, dancing, dancing.

On Monday Cher comes by for the last of her stuff, a shirt, a sock, the other earring. She puts her finger against her lips, *shhh*, but Mom hears, all, "At least take some soup, here's a Tupperware," and then also with the phonebook open to the section on annulments, "It's not too late!"

"Who gives advice?" Cher says. "That can't even come to a wedding in the first place?"

Mom makes a face like Pearl Harbor morning plus *60 Minutes* being cancelled. Jonelle crosses her chest and spits on the floor, some eye hex even Gypsies don't believe in. "You and your tore-up husband, *pffft.*"

"Wait, what?" Cher says, laughs.

Jonelle reaches into the sink and throws the clear disc that usually spins in the microwave but is currently soaking even though the atomized noodles and beans are impervious to hot water. It digs into the wall and then hits a stud.

The sound of glass.

Doors slam. Upstairs and downstairs.

Dilly Jr. starts to cry.

I sweep him up and press him tight against my chest. It's possible he's actually scared, has some internal meter that senses turbulence, but I think he just wants a hot dog and a ball and some soda and to take off his pants and throw rocks and scream with pure milky glee, so totally ready to evolve into a tool of nonstop motion and fun.

FOR A WHOLE YEAR stories waft around, different characters, different versions, *Cher did this* or *Butterfly did that.* How they're the reason all those cats are missing. How Cher gained a hundred pounds and carries a TEC-9 in her purse. How Butterfly keeps monkey heads floating in pickle jars on a shelf made of bones.

Dilly Jr. doesn't care. He's busy learning. Up and around, trembly thighs and then step, step, flop. He's got six hairs and two teeth, top and bottom, little choppers that bite my knuckle, ravenous with love.

After Christmas Mom gets sick.

Just a bit and then really. The doctors at first are all tubes and pills and *Press here for the nurse*, but after a while, practically, *You might as well just go home, we could use the bed*. The night she passes, Mom puts her hand on my neck and whispers that she loves me. I love her, too. Always has. Same here. I'm a good boy. Only because she made me be. Great things are coming. How badly I wish she could be there to see them.

The last thing is Tucson.

The church next to the plot next to her grandfather's headstone, where she intends to be buried.

I promise her, absolutely, if that's what you want.

THEY SEND THE BODY ahead on a refrigerated train, and who knew such a thing could be paid for or even existed? Then on Friday, Wade and Cher glide up in a new Buick. Jonelle refuses to go. "Fifteen hours? In a car? With them?"

"But it's my mother."

"Exactly."

I put on my wedding suit and slip into the backseat, Cher with her hair up, a deeper red than usual, like it's been dipped in the Ganges.

"Sucks and all, homes," Wade says, a license to say stupid things since he's covering gas. "But I liked your mother. She had style."

Cher rolls her eyes. "Guess what Mr. High Roller did. Mr. Top of the Line? Just guess."

When I don't answer, she holds up a bouquet of flowers, shows the side of the wrapper that says, COMPLIMENTS OF AMAYZING GRACE AND GROCERY!

It's quiet all the way to the interstate and then Wade goes, "Hey, Dillard?"

"Yeah?"

"Buckle the fuck up."

And so I do.

JUST OVER THE BORDER a hose comes loose and we're towed to the station. By the time it's fixed we're late for the viewing and Tucson is still two hundred miles, nothing but desert and the radio, *I'm a cowboy* and *On a steel horse I ride.*

"Man, you'd pound your nuts to jelly on a steel horse," Wade says.

The funeral home's dark, door locked. Cher hits the horn *beep* and then the door *bang* until a janitor comes to the window, some Russian waving his mop. "Is to close, you see? Is not open." Wade flashes him a ten and then a twenty and then three twenties. The Russian lets us in. Red carpet and curtains and ceilings. Way in back, Mom. Still in her coffin, all powder and rouge, I never once in my life saw her wear makeup. She looks like someone graffitied her, THIS EXIT FOR REAL NATIVE CRAFTS!

"Sorry, Dillard," Wade says, then goes and sits in the car.

It seems so dumb, tears. I wipe them from Dilly Jr.'s cheeks every day like they're nothing.

"Shhh," Cher says, nails on the back of my neck, tall in black stilettos. I nod and she scratches, a sing-song of mourning and comfort that somehow feels older than either of us. I put the flowers on the casket, too long in the car and now a powder gray. Cher fixes Mom's dress but leaves her shoes, which are on the wrong feet. Upstairs there's the sound of one of those floor buffers, a rotary thing that crosses the planks in wide, reverent arcs.

"Why?" I ask.

"I guess it was just her time."

"No. Not that."

Cher makes a face. "I'm *Dilly*. Explain the *world* to me."

"Not the world. Just Butterfly."

She pokes me in the chest, hard.

"Because I didn't want to come in second or third, okay Dillard?"

"What did you want?"

"To come in worst."

She leans over. I'm shoved up against the casket. There's a commiserating brush of lips. A sisterly acknowledgment of our mutual loss. For two beats. Three. Then the time to separate comes and goes. She moves closer. Cautiously exploring. It's like being ten again, because all my friends were right. I *did* watch her take a shower, since she always pushed the curtain aside. There *were* special games in the basement, almost never a winner.

We say nothing, send messages like we used to, when words were for parents and teachers and friends too dumb to know an entire life existed beyond homework and sneakers and bikes, too busy talking shit and throwing punches that wouldn't matter until they gained fifty pounds. I never wanted any part of the thefts and lies and fights because there was always the plaid couch against the far wall, the broken lamp, me and Cher giggling while Mom chuffed around upstairs, calling our names.

She pulls me closer, tap tap tap with the point of her tongue. I send gentle replies, like walking heel-toe toward a deer on the lawn. Slowly, slowly. Careful not to spook. Pull aside a branch. Wait for it to sniff the air, go back to chewing leaves.

I open my eyes. Hers are closed.

I absorb the pressure of her lips, the heat of her everything.

"Dilly," she whispers, and somehow hearing my name collapses a scaffold of restraint that had already begun to buckle.

I run my hands up her sides, under her dress, too hard, too fast.

"Jesus," she says, spins away.

"Wait."

The door slams.

I wipe lipstick from my chin, thinking it's weird how almost everyone does the worst thing, every time. Gives in to their essential natures without thought or complaint. Our little brains suckered by the first shiny thing. And then, when we have a chance not to be, a real and obvious chance to prove we're actually half-human, still fuck it up.

I'm looking at Mom when the Russian cracks the door. "Finish?"

"Yeah."

He holds out his hand. "You want to see another, is sixty dollars."

THE BURIAL IS SHORT and quick, the priest drunk or in a hurry.

Ashes to ashes and so forth amen.

Handfuls of dirt, palms dried on slacks.

A walk along a gravel path.

AT THE BORDER we stop at a Tas-T-Grill. Cher leans against the car with a cigarette, one long line of smoke floating straight up, like there hasn't been any wind in the desert for a hundred years.

"You coming?" Wade asks.

No answer.

"You want me to get you something?"

No answer.

There's a plastic table under a plastic umbrella. It's too small. We slap down trays, touch knees. I'd forgotten what it was like to watch Wade eat, the stop-motion animation from scalp to cleft, the butterfly dancing from cheek to cheek.

"Something on your mind, Dillard?"

"No."

"You sure? Now's your chance. Dead mommy buys you a one-time pass."

"For what?"

"Being way too honest without I'm kicking your ass after."

A family comes and sits. The kids stare, get scolded. They get up, decide to eat in the car after all.

"I guess I have been thinking."

"Proceed."

"Just how you should get out before you get busted."

"Yeah? You worried about my career prospects?"

"Maybe head back down to Santa Monica or whatever. Stay one step ahead."

He starts in on the second burger. "So I can sling drinks for drunk frats? Pocket wet quarters like you?"

"No one leaves change anymore."

"Or, hey, maybe I could go back to school. Volunteer on weekends. *Listen, kids, don't forget that everyone's special in their own special way.*"

A pair of hornets crawl around the edge of his soda. One falls in.

"I didn't say school."

"You're right. My apologies. But here's what I'm wondering. In this scenario where I hit the bricks, does Cher happen to stay behind?"

"How should I know?"

"Yeah, I guess I can see how it'd play out. Her all sad without me around, figures it's probably time to move back on over to Dilly's place."

I try to get up, but he slides forward, pins me against the bench. It hurts.

"Anything else you need to get off your chest?"

"No."

"You're making a really weird face."

"Stop."

He pushes harder. "Why? Something wrong?"

I take a swing that misses, scrape my knuckles on the table.

Wade smiles, lets go. We're six inches apart. His scar seems angrier with the sun directly above, looks like spilled tea, burned and peeled away, again and again.

"Hey, Dilly, you think you could carry this weight?" He runs his fingers gently around the wings, knows exactly where the perimeter is. "You got the shoulders for this?"

He's right. I would have folded a long time ago.

"No. But at least you've got my sister."

"You dumb shit. No one has your sister."

We motor through the night, without a word, and then drop Wade just outside town.

"I got business."

He hands me the keys. I adjust the seat. There's no traffic for once. We're almost at their place when I'm finally like, "Hey, you wanna get a beer or something?"

"No."

"No?"

"But maybe coffee."

I find a spot and then a booth. Cher orders two donuts. The cooks watch and wish, press themselves against the counter, never bring my tea.

"Well?" She says.

I know there's an important question full of layers and meaning. A statement or an apology, I'm *so so so* whatever. But it's like how I always laugh instead of being the one who makes the joke. How I stand and watch while someone else puts out the fire, rescues the baby. I've always known I'd have exactly the life I do. *That Dilly, he's a good guy,* everyone slapping my back and picking me for their team and inviting me to the movies first even though there were better, cooler people, but at least with me there'd never be any surprises.

She licks her fingers.

"It wasn't a monkey, it was a capuchin."

"Huh?"

"All these years we've been saying monkey. That's fucked up, don't you think?"

"I guess."

"You know, those first nights after I came back, I kept thinking you were secretly winking at me. Like you were acting dumb, but still in on the game. All *Where you been? What was it like?* And so I figured one night you'd finally break down, laugh in my face. But you just sat there sucking your thumb."

"I never sucked my thumb."

"You know what an analogy is, Dillard?"

"A fancy word for none of it was real?"

"Exactly."

"What about L.A.?"

"I mean, it exists."

"What about Terrence?"

"He runs a dozen websites. Guess what kind?"

"But we went to his agency. He gave us Moët."

Cher stands, drops three dollars on the table, leans close enough that I can smell myself on her.

"I mean seriously, Dillard. Who in fuck ever heard of a school for models?"

It's maybe a year later and we're sitting in the kitchen. Dilly Jr. is under the table going *vroom vroom* with his little cars and *grr grr* with his little bears. I have the morning shift, since Manny had a stroke Fourth of July and bumped me up to manager. First thing, I got rid of all the Christmas lights and beer signs, the pinball and ashtrays. Put a little stage in the corner. We have live music, trivia, rich-fucker whiskey. Cute girls bringing drinks to dudes who come in for the drinks and cute girls.

I'm talking to the guy owns the building about maybe buying the place.

Jonelle can't believe what's gotten into me.

I'm like, "Nothing's gotten in, it's gotten loose."

She shakes her ass, winks, says, "Daddy, I know that's right."

Then we let Dilly Jr. watch *Curious George* for a while, lock the door.

But not this morning.

She kisses my neck, slides the paper next to my eggs.

"Sorry, babe, but you should probably read this first."

It's in the metro section, no picture. The whole thing only rates half a column. Someone unbeknownst to authorities shot someone beknownst to authorities, a certain Wade "Butterfly" Belkowitz. In fact, they shot him four times and then stole his little triangles in what authorities are referring to as possibly drug-related. There's a mention of Stu Mayse, second chances, the collapse of the social safety net, some editorializing about the takers not the makers in this world.

No warning about keeping monkeys as pets.

We don't go to the funeral.

I try to call Cher but no one answers for a long time, and when they do it's someone pretending they don't speak English but in any case understanding enough to tell me she hasn't been there in months.

"What did you expect?" Jonelle asks, takes the paper away, combs my hair. I can feel her belly, getting bigger again, pressed against my back.

"Nothing. It's why I'm never disappointed."

Dilly Jr. crawls into my lap, makes his time-for-snack face.

"Did you know Mommy married a philosophy professor?" Jonelle asks.

He actually considers.

"No."

"Well, honey, neither did I."

D.C. Metro

There's just no way Penny can hack crashing another squat. With the incessant house meetings, the humorless stances on bacon and Kurdistan and stripper poles. The weird rules like *no using the soup pan to cook freebase* or *stay off the hammock after dark*. Who gets kicked out of a squat, anyway? Who has the power to make unilateral decisions in what is theoretically a leaderless community of equals? Penny has no idea who stole the money, but Sad Girl is still pissed. Razr and Roy Boi say they're gonna kick Penny's ass if she even thinks about coming around again, tries to sneak into a show.

Fine.

Shows are boring now anyway. Too expensive, full of teeny-boppers and rock stars, the scene nowhere near as cool as it used to be. Besides, Penny's psychic, knows she's gonna find a place soon, a home always on the horizon of her mind.

And she's right.

Even if it turns out to be a gentrifier's brownstone owned by two men who cook together and sleep together and listen to Dakota Staton records while homemaking preserves. Jack and Francis. Except Francis calls himself "Jill" and waits for people to laugh, which you could pretty easily decide is unbearable. Or you could just roll with it, since it's a renter's market and Penny has zero other options. Mainly because she rocks shaved sidewalls and inky bangs, calf-high Docs laced tight. No makeup except blood-red lipstick, always. A Slayer tat competing with skulls and cue balls across tiny, sleeveless arms.

If she weighs a hundred pounds, it's mostly steel-toe.

What the hell is everyone so scared of?

For six weeks Penelope (known as Penny Laid in the last band she screamed for) has answered ads, seeped trustworthiness, lied about the security deposit she doesn't have. She's been shined off by Georgetown couples with *this-closet-is-a-bedroom* smiles and *you'll-end-up-babysitting-us* toddlers. She's been passed on by coder geeks sunk deep in crushed empties and multiplayer action. But it's the older women who sting the most. With their frowns and armfuls of cat-calendar cats, with their arid infertility and smell of no one emptying the hair trap in the Roomba since last August.

"We'll call you," they say.

"Doubt it," Penny answers, getting pre-emptive her signature move in the face of disappointment. "I gave you a fake number anyhow."

So when she sees the little red smiley face on the index card at the church she never goes to and then takes the bus all the way out to Race Riot Central, halfway down a street that's practically Lebanon except crack instead of religion, and then gets off right where Jack and Francis wait on a brick stoop holding hands like the twin princes of wearing matching sweaters just to fuck with all the humorless young queens who think they're cutting edge, it's way too weird and perfect to say no.

Yes!

Penny puts down her guitar cases in the front hall. One with a guitar in it and the other full of lipstick, underwear, and her tarot deck.

"Well, I guess that just means more shelf space for me," Francis says.

"Don't listen to him, minimalism is the new maximalism," Jack says.

Penny unpacks, opens the bedroom window, can barely breathe. Her latest psychic flash: D.C. is hot. The temperature rises way up over a hundred like it's proud of itself. She shuffles her tarot, draws the Irradiated Sun and then the Rascally Nubian, decides to take a walk through the neighborhood. It's a forgotten triangle off Rhode Island Ave, a couple acres of blacktop and rotting trash that the hibachi-tenders and forty-guzzlers who holla at her every step call New Jack Shitty.

They say, "Hey, white girl, what you doin' uptown?"

They say, "Hey, Trixie, you lost?"

They say, "Hey, punk rawk, lemme buy you a drink."

No thanks, fellas, but I appreciate the warm welcome!

When she gets back, Jack and Francis are coloring Shrinky Dinks they found at the farmers' market.

"Hey, Penny," Francis calls, "I got markers for you, too."

"They're the sniff kind," Jack says. "You have to try Mango Surprise."

Penny takes the stairs two at a time, tells herself, *The boys are talking, you should answer them.*

Penny tells herself, *Communication is the cornerstone of a happy household.*

Penny tells herself, *And besides, when's the last time someone bought you Magic Markers?*

Since the answer is never, she resolves to go back down and lean against the cutting board, gush about how great it is to have new friends plus a door that actually locks. But maybe first take a shower and then brush her teeth with Jack's imported Sri Lankan toothpaste that tastes like saffron and Tamil blood.

Penny throws the wet towel on the carpet, picks a pair of fresh overalls. It's punishing to wear black in the equatorial heat, and so her wardrobe long ago transitioned from tights and leather to a daily pair of white painter's overalls that allow maximum wicking of perspiration even if they make her look like an extra from a Dexys Midnight Runners video. Besides, she's so small and stridently vegan that her sweat smells clean and untoxic, sort of like apple puree, like maybe she should bottle it and sell it online to Okinawa business pervs for three grand an ounce.

Downstairs, Francis bangs a cowbell with a spoon, partly because of a joke about Blue Öyster Cult that she doesn't understand and partly because every Thursday is roommate dinner night.

"Hey, señorita, grub's ready!"

There are salads and wine and experimental things on crackers. Billie Holiday alternates with Édith Piaf. Francis leans across the table, face flushed, two glasses in on a merlot with an overdesigned label. He's tall with glasses and wavy bangs, a lawyer for a nonprofit that defends black people in situations where it probably would have been smarter to be white. Jack is a therapist. He has a tiny blond mustache and specializes in body relevance issues. They just want to make it official that they totally get Penny's aesthetic. All she needs is a direction. Francis thinks she should apply to architectural school. Jack thinks she should start an all-girl band that's essentially the D.C. Pussy Riot, except not Russian and with a different name because people are so uptight these days, "May I offer into evidence Janet Jackson's flabby little tit?"

There are so many reasons for Penny to be annoyed.

To feel dismissive and superior in an abrasive way that will eventually lead to being kicked to the curb, guitar case flung open in the middle of the street *and forget about your deposit, gutter punk!*

Instead she finds that on most nights she loves the boys unreservedly.

Like when they open mail together in the front hall after work, make fun of catalogs.

Or haggle at the farmers' market with the old woman who looks like a candied yam.

Or huddle under the afghan, crunch spice-infused popcorn all through *Houseboat* with Cary Grant, then tear *Inception* a new ass, not only because that shit made *zero* sense, but Leo the Cap is totally overrated!

By summer, Penny can't wait to come home each day and do something fun. Like make aprons out of oven mitts, or play Risk for a nickel an annexation. She comes to depend on Francis and Jack for all number and variety of familial experiences heretofore unfurnished or even subconsciously recognized as lacking, which include long, supportive talks about her boyfriendlessness and the possibility that she could meet a cute little Martha or a Susan instead, no one would judge. Not to mention regular rent extensions, which Francis is 77 percent cool about and tends to remind her of in a ridiculous cowboy accent, *It's check writin' time, darlin'*. Penny is totally paying what she owes. Which is 2.6 months' rent. She's good for it. Really. She has a job doesn't she? Of course she does. At a deli called Food 4 Thought where all the sandwiches are named after famous people. Like the Andy Warhol is an open-faced beef. The Bo Diddley is spiced ham. The Sarah Palin is mayo on white, which Penny thinks only dolts still laugh at, like shooting fish in a performance art piece about fish shooting.

But then on the morning she's about to run down and

jump in their bed, give Jack a tarot reading on the coverlet that's so soft it feels like unborn orphan rhino skin, which is what vicuna actually is or maybe Francis was joking, she accidentally drops her deck on the floor.

Lying exposed, the Emperor of Meat.

Which means the boys are taking a trip.

Penny hates being alone, hates announcements.

Ten minutes later Jack and Francis sit her down for a big announcement.

"We're taking a trip!"

She shuffles the deck again.

The Collector of Cups.

Which means they also intend to acquire half the remaining trinkets of the ancient world and crate them back to D.C. in order to assemble a display of sometimes cursed and other times simply overpriced artifacts that will span two rooms and every remaining empty shelf.

"Where?"

Jack unfolds a "Welcome to Istanbul" brochure. There are fabulous arrays of tiles and minarets and invigorating spa treatment packages. A gorgeous green pool stretches to the horizon line above a city Alexander the Great once conquered, or at least aggressively visited. Penny can taste danger at the tip of her tongue, which is where she's most psychic. Pure frozen metal. Sand fleas and pipe bombs and every fifth tuk-tuk driver wearing a suicide vest. But she doesn't have the words to warn or explain. And if she tells them how she knows what she knows, the boys might stop thinking it's a coincidence she wins at every board game, knows every answer, maybe even mind-melded them into letting her move in to begin with.

Besides, she's proud of how proud they are of their *extemporaneousness,* which in itself is a word three vowels and four syllables too long to argue with.

Penny reaches down, turns over the Curiously Aroused Brigand.

At least she won't be alone.

"When?"

"Next week," they say, click imaginary glasses.

PENNY HOLDS HER shit together for six and a half days.

It's not so much the heat as the humidity.

It's not so much the impending as the doom.

Her mood is lethal, like a hole's been cored in her forehead, vital prefrontal bits vacuumed out and a grim sludge poured back in.

C'mon, girl, make it work!

She can't.

It's gonna be okay!

It's not.

The phone's about to ring!

No shit.

"Penelope? Phone!" Francis calls, rolling his carry on carefully over the sustainable hardwood. For some reason there's an extension in the upstairs bathroom, mounted above the toilet. Penny slides from a knot of sofa pillows, her

cellphone cut off because she never really sent in the first payment let alone all the other ones, so she's stuck with the land
line, although is fairly sure no one has the number. Not even
work. Not even Mom, who might have died two years ago,
and definitely not Dad, who was, basically, theoretical.

She lines the toilet seat with strips of Charmin, picks up
the receiver.

"Hello?"

"Penny Laid!"

"What?"

"Hey, relax. It's Kurt."

"I know who it is."

"Cool. What you been up to?"

What she's been up to is reading a lot of philosophy. Kant.
Leibniz. Husserl. Jack owns many, many books, and because
of the views of various morose Germans, Penny has come
under the thrall of the idea that meaning is relative. Or that
everything is relatively meaningless. It's a theory supported
by generations of doctrine and precept, as well as the fact
that she fucked Kurt in the utility closet at work two days ago.

And then spent the night reeling in a priori mortification.

Even if it wasn't fucked exactly. Not dictionary fucked,
but definitely parts of him inside of parts of her.

"I don't have a raincoat," he'd said, grinning. "So let's just
play some games."

Games?

The word had made her want to howl at the planet and
all the things wrong with it, the very worst of them being

how everything was so appallingly casual. She almost made it through the next shift by pretending there *were* no games, let alone ones that had been played, when Kurt pinched her ass in front of a regular.

If there were a tarot for Groper Never Gropes Again, she would have whipped it out and kabobed it to his chest.

Instead she botched a meatball Bebe Rebozo, toasted a Timberlake, slathered gravy on a Kate Moss, and then made the Truman Capote with corned beef instead of cold blood. Or no, wait, salmon spread. The waitresses began to complain. They already hated Penny as it was, mainly since she never wore a bra, which was number one-through-five on the list of Ten Things That Will Make a Waitress Immediately Hate You, even though she only got stares from boys who liked girls who looked like gutter punk boys, so where was the competition? Penny had tried to be friends, admired how the waitresses counted their greasy tips twice and made jokes about their endless periods and all had toddlers named Liam or Conner that they failed to hurry home to at the end of every shift.

But the haters weren't having it.

Food 4 Thought's manager, who everyone called Uncle, finally shook his big gray dreadlock head and told Penny he had no choice but to put her on probation, *Due to an avalanche of poorly constructed sandwiches plus staff unrest.* Which basically meant she was demoted to condiments for the foreseeable future.

It was total bullshit.

Or totally deserved.

One of them for sure.

"I'M NOT UP TO anything," Penny says, releases a stream of hot pee. "Okay, Kurt?"

"Fine. What are you so grumpy for?"

"I just found weevils in my Cheerios."

It'd actually happened a few days ago. Six of them wiggling in the milk. A portent. Evil Weevil was a rare card, delivered only one message: chaos. Penny screamed and dropped the bowl. Francis rubbed her shoulders while Jack cleaned it up.

"Harsh. You okay?"

"No."

"What's all that noise?"

All that noise was the taxi to the airport, the driver carelessly banging Jack's matching brushed-chrome Vuittons down the lacquered steps.

"My roommates are going on a trip."

"Where?"

"Jersey City. I gotta go. I'm gonna be late for work."

"Hold on. I was thinking maybe I could swing by. We need to talk."

There's a vintage Mr. Spock clock on the wall, his pointy right ear the minute hand.

Not a good idea, Spock says. *You're already on thin ice.*

"Not a good idea," Penny says. "I'm already on thin ice."

"Nah, Uncle's cool. I'll bring beer. We'll go in late together, tell him there was a bus strike."

Penny still hasn't figured out why she let Kurt take her into the stock room to begin with. Unless it was to punish Jack and Francis. Unless it was because she dreaded being alone, even for an hour, stuck in the big echoing house with all eight thousand framed pictures vying for her attention.

On the other hand, maybe *she* was the one who grabbed Kurt's elbow. Maybe she was the one who winked and tossed the bolt, mashed him against sixty pounds of red onions, the Imbecile's Seduction, strains of imaginary flute punctuated by cooks hammering at the door.

Kurt, with his way-blasé hair and trigger grin.

Kurt who really does smell like teen spirit.

Kurt, who takes arty portraits with discontinued film stocks, who was born to be in the liner notes, who probably owns a shiny kayak and has an interview lined up at that new animation studio down by the water.

"I don't want to," Penny says.

"C'mon. Why not?"

"I don't like you very much."

He laughs. "Yeah, right."

"No, for real. You need to shave your stubble. It's so obvious. And wear less-tight shirts."

"Hang on, let me write these down."

The Charmin has turned to gum beneath Penny's sweaty thighs. She puts down the receiver and goes to her room, where her sister's picture is tacked above the bed.

May looks annoyed. *Asking for trouble, as usual.*

Penny loves May, but girlfriend has her own problems. Like for instance no husband and then two feral boys who eat a pound of macadamia brittle a day and refer to their sister as "Stink Crevice."

Joel is older now. Todd sees a professional on Fridays. But forget that, you're gonna get yourself canned.

Penny has lost plenty of jobs before, but she likes Food 4 Thought. She even likes Uncle, who was mean about the condiments but has a big belly and rainbow suspenders and nips off a flask of Southern Comfort while telling funny stories about once being a roadie for Canned Heat. On the other hand, it's only a matter of time before she gets fired anyway, some cash or expensive knife set will go missing and she'll be too easy not to blame.

You want to start looking for another place to live? How'd that work out last time?

"Crappy," Penny says.

Then why take the chance?

Because Rousseau said that all is chaos and contentment is death.

Because Locke said that men deserve reparations for the injustice of their labors.

Because Penny's framed picture of David Lee Roth does a scissor kick and gives her a raging thumbs-up.

It's party time! Go for it, babe!

Only a fool ignores Diamond Dave.

Penny has forty minutes to get dressed and make her

shift. She puts on a double-coat of lipstick, goes back to the bathroom, and picks up the phone.

With any luck he hung up, Spock says.

"You there?"

"Yeah, baby," Kurt says.

"I'll be ready in twenty minutes."

"Righteous."

"But if you say righteous again, it's off."

"Solid."

"Same."

"Okay, okay, Jesus."

Penny hangs up and goes downstairs to say good-bye to the boys.

KURT TAKES IN the brownstone's facade, whistles. He's wearing chinos and a dirty shirt. Lean, unshowered. A cook's hands. Grill burns. Forearms all veins, an interstate from wrist to throat.

"Sweet place. And let me get this straight, you kick it with two dudes?"

"I thought you were bringing beer."

"I said we'd go get some."

"No, you didn't. Besides, it's too hot to walk to the grocery store."

"Walking's for the impoverished underbelly. Anyone owns this place definitely has a ride."

It's true. Twin Volvos. Jack pressed the keys to the blue one into Penny's hand before getting in the cab, stage-whispered, *Only for emergencies, chica!*

"They don't drive."

Kurt winks. "You sure?"

For a second she hates him with the strength of a thousand dying suns.

Then it passes.

"Fine. It's parked around back."

Kurt adjusts the mirror, ejects the CD from the player, flings it into traffic.

"Not cool."

"I know, but seriously, *Seven and the Ragged Tiger*?"

They go a dozen blocks, pull into the empty lot with a chirp. There are crackheads and drunks. Fondlers and purse snatchers. And then just people.

"Safeway's probably safer," Penny says.

"We're already here," Kurt says.

The market smells like a complaint to the lettuce distributor. An old guy in a bloody apron chops at something that might be fish, *slit slit slit*. There's a nudie calendar on the wall, the kind auto parts companies send out for free. July looks like Angela Davis. She gives Penny a wink, *How'd you like a taste of this, honey?*

"I don't swing that way."

"What?" Kurt says.

Penny flips open her tarot deck. Little Boy Lost.

A little boy tears around the corner, slides to a stop.

He's wearing thick glasses, shirtless, chest heaving.

Penny offers him a grape.

"That washed?" his mother asks, forces her cart between them.

"No."

"Then what you giving it to him for?"

Penny sniffs the grape, puts it back.

"I dunno."

"That's right, you don't."

"Shit," Kurt says, hefts a case of beer. "I forgot my wallet."

"You gettin' paper 'cause we out of plastic," the register girl says, rings them up.

AT THE FAR END of the parking lot a guy leans in the Volvo's window, broken glass at his feet.

"The fuck?" Kurt says.

The guy turns, a tire iron in one hand. He's wearing orange shorts and Timberlands, beard shaved so precisely it looks drawn on with marker.

"Oh, man, is this your ride? No wonder my key don't work."

"Fight!" someone yells.

A pack of teenagers amble over to watch, hands in pockets and backward visors. Some wear big nylon coats, frowning under the sun.

"Not cool, Sinbad," Kurt says.

"Kick his ass, Lavelle," a girl with blue lips says.

"Let's just go," Penny says.

Someone throws a bottle. Kurt puts up his fists, circles left as a cruiser speeds into the lot. The old guy in the bloody apron points from behind glass doors. A blip of siren sends the crowd in every direction. Half walk off with a mannered lope: *fuck you*. The rest run, flat out, into the alley.

"There a problem?" the cop asks.

"Negative," Kurt says. "Locked our keys in the car. Dude here was helping out."

The cop in the passenger's seat laughs.

"Don't you think you boys are on the wrong side of the river?"

"No, sir," Kurt says.

"I'm not a boy," Penny says.

"You got ID, Mr. Goodwrench?"

"You bet," Lavelle says, reaches for his wallet.

The cop waves it off, gets in the cruiser, guns back into traffic.

"Hey rock star," Lavelle says. "I owe you one."

Kurt reaches into the car and rolls down what's left of the window. "More than one."

"No, for real. Sorry about that."

Penny likes Lavelle's unhurried voice, his stance, thinks maybe he used to be a soldier. Sprayed the desert with bullets, never hit anything. Was yelled at, yelled back. Got that girl in the auto pool pregnant, got discharged, has a whole life full of actual experiences instead of just ironic jokes and opinions about movies.

"It's okay," Penny says.

"No, it isn't," Kurt says. "This is gonna run at least eighty bucks."

"It's not even his car," Penny says.

"Oh no?" Lavelle says.

"He's not even in a band," Penny says.

"Who said I was in a band?" Kurt says.

Penny cuts the deck. The Consigliere of Selma. Lavelle has a gold hoop in his left ear, just like the guy in the picture. She leans down and sweeps up a handful of safety glass. The shards are beveled, refract the asphalt a dirty pink.

"I seriously want to take a bath in these."

Lavelle laughs. "You one of those sensitive arty chicks, huh? All full up on deep thoughts?"

Penny wonders if not answering is a confirmation or denial. Voltaire once said all language was an elitist ruse. On the other hand, Voltaire was a dead French asshole and Penny was here, now, in an empty parking lot with a very large man. And Kurt.

"Can I ask you a question?"

"Shoot."

She points to the car.

"Were you gonna drive it to a chop shop?"

Lavelle shakes his head. "You been watching too many movies, slim. No such thing. Honestly? I was just hoping you had a couple twenties in the glove. My experience being, most Volvos do."

"Okay, we are officially exchanging thief tips with the guy who broke into our car," Kurt says. "Just for the record."

"You party, rock star?"

Kurt frowns. "Maybe."

Lavelle writes his number on the back of a coupon.

"You leave a message here, I hook you up with a little weed. The dank. Just so we straight."

"That's sweet," Penny says.

"Sweet?" Kurt says.

"Y'all talk like an old couple, you know it?"

"We're just friends," Penny says.

"Well, this has been awesome," Kurt says, as some of the teenagers straggle back. "Diplomacy. The uniting of cultures and whatnot." He takes Penny's hand, gets her into the passenger seat. "But we gotta split."

Lavelle hikes up his shorts. "I was you, I would, too. Assuming I would ever be you, which I wouldn't. But still."

"Bye," Penny says.

Kurt flashes the peace sign, peels away.

THE BACKYARD IS ten feet of cement surrounded by a rusty fence. Kurt turns over an old plastic kiddie pool, fills it with a hose, then drags out most of the sectional, a suede L that Jack calls his Burgundy Mistress.

Penny finds a terry robe in Francis's closet, attaches her wallet chain, pure gangster. Kurt strips to his Calvins. They pop beers, soak their feet.

Penny hasn't been swimming in, what, six years? She was good once, a wisp in the water, fast and light. They'd practically begged her to join the school team, try out for state's.

Or wait, that isn't true. Penny hates swimming. She almost drowned in a lake in Kentucky that time her stepfather, really just some guy named Jim who always burned the hot dogs, grabbed her and May by the armpits and threw them in, laughed as they stroked and flailed, covered in rotted leaves and mud.

Kurt extends his legs, rubs his feet against hers.

"So let's talk about the other day."

Penny cuts her deck. The Time Machine That's Actually a Cardboard Box.

"There was no other day."

"Will you drop the shit for second? I mean, listen, I get your thing. Alternachick against the world? Hates everything almost as much as she hates herself? That's cool. Not too original, but whatever."

The phone rings.

"That's probably work," Penny says.

Kurt runs his hand past her knee, lets it rest just beneath the hem of her robe. She's not wearing a bathing suit. Mostly because she doesn't have one.

"But you know what? It's okay to let someone like you. Me, for instance. Punk's not gonna kick you out of the club."

Penny gets up, yanks open the glass door. There's an office in the basement, which is damp and slightly cooler than the rest of the house. She tiptoes down the wooden steps, sits at the desk.

I don't think Jack would like your wet clompers on the mahogany, Francis says.

Framed pictures of the boys line the far wall. In a convertible smiling, in the kitchen smiling, hilariously knocked over by waves. Jack nods in a reindeer sweater, expectantly under mistletoe.

He's right. I don't like it at all.

Penny puts her feet down. "Sorry."

To be honest, hon? I'm not super happy with the way things are going in general.

Seriously, Francis says. *How long have we been gone? A couple hours and already it's* Risky Business?

"I know, I know."

And let's be real, you're no Rebecca De Mornay.

"You don't have to be mean about it."

Jack sighs from a selfie. *Listen, hon, Rough Trade out there may talk a good game, but you better believe he only wants one thing.*

Yeah, Francis says. *Did you at least buy some protection?*

"No."

Bad planning, Jack says.

"There's nothing to plan for."

Why, because you can't get preggo? Haven't you had your first period yet?

"Hey," Penny says.

You are awfully skinny. I recommend raw fish. Maybe a bowl of Triscuits and some niacin.

"That's none of your business!"

Don't get all exercised. We're just trying to—

Kurt calls down the stairs.

"Trying to what?"

"Wrong number," Penny says.

"You coming back up?"

"In a minute."

BY EIGHT THE kiddie pool has a dozen beer bottles swaying at the bottom. The new Descendents album cranks through the stereo, six components in an oak rack.

Penny finds Kurt in the kitchen.

"I didn't say it was okay to have a party."

"You didn't say it wasn't. Or wait, maybe you weren't around to ask."

He turns to talk to the waitress who always wears the red shirt that shows off the red bra. Most of Food 4 Thought stands around drinking beer. Cooks and busboys talk shit, take turns shoving each other into counters and against the stove. Two register girls make out on the patio. White smoke blows from the grill, a dishwasher with purple hair adding stuff to the flames: a glove, some magazines, *The Collected Bizet*.

Penny finds Uncle in the hall, admiring a set of figurines depicting the all stars of Czarist Russia.

"We really should have a Rasputin sandwich," he says.

In the living room there's the three-tiered sound of broken glass.

Uncle snaps his suspenders. "I'm guessing that's a mirror?"

They go to look. On the floor are fragments of red and black.

Was it the tea set? Francis asks, from a picture of Francis sipping tea.

"Yeah," Penny says.

"Yeah, what?" Uncle says.

The world is now a less civilized place, Jack says.

Penny collects most of a saucer, holds the delicate shards in her palm.

"Maybe I can glue it back together?"

"I doubt it," Uncle says.

Listen to Pollyanna.

Penny yanks Francis off the wall, slaps him face down. "You're dead or blown up anyway. What difference does it make?"

What do you mean? Jack says. *We're having cocktails. We're having dinner on a ship floating down the Bosphorus.*

"Nope. You're never coming back."

So not true, sweetie. Who told you that?

"Only every card in the deck."

Francis says something, his voice too muffled to understand. Uncle isn't there at all.

AT MIDNIGHT AN SUV pulls into the driveway.

Penny opens the door. "What are you doing here?"

"Your boy says y'all got a rager going."

Kurt shrugs. "You got that weed?"

Lavelle lights a joint, inspects the stereo rack. The Descendents cut out. Wu-Tang cuts in. Half of Food 4 Thought grab their jackets, hit the street.

"Lame," Kurt says.

"Don't fear the natives," Lavelle says.

Penny cuts the tarot, pulls the Vaginocracy.

"Can't have a party without women," Lavelle says, picks up the phone.

Within an hour sixty people dance in a sweaty mass in the living room. Others stagger around in groups, yelling. Three guys take turns throwing the same girl into the pool. One of them fishes her out and then they do it again.

Penny sinks next to Lavelle on the couch. They clink beers.

"This really y'all's house?"

"Yeah."

"Don't take it the wrong way, but you don't strike me as the lady entrepreneur type. Your Martha Stewarts and such."

"I'm one of those trust fund punks you read so much about."

He laughs. "Can I ask you something?"

"Shoot."

"You really think I look like Sinbad?"

Penny pictures the guy on stage, goatee, sweatpants, never once funny.

"Who?"

Lavelle seems pleased by her answer. They both watch Kurt dance in the corner with an incredibly tall woman. He's all sweat, shirt half off. The woman wears a sarong, bangles, a headdress. She looks like Sudanese royalty.

"Now, I like your boy and all, but there's no way in god's green kingdom he can handle that."

The woman sways, imperceptibly, as Kurt bungles around her.

"Sinbad to the rescue," Lavelle says, and then dances his way in.

PENNY WAKES CURLED into a ball, shivers, the air conditioner on high. She tries to remember why she's in a closet. At some point there was an argument. Something broke. She climbed up and away from it, remembered the space just off the attic full of used modems and never-sent birthday presents, back massagers and socket sets, slid behind a pile of old coats and let the weight of the beer drape over her like one of those heavy aprons they give you when they're about to X-ray every last tooth in your head.

Next to her are Kurt's socks.

Grey with green stripes.

Penny tries to rewind the videotape, nothing but static and muffled voices.

Pulls a card, the Prefrontal Blank.

Jack's bathrobe sweeps the staircase clean behind her. Most of the furniture in the living room is on its side, plants knocked over, cans and bottles leaning against themselves. The stereo's gone, maybe some other stuff. Not too bad. The broken wine rack sucks though, Merlot seeping into the carpet.

"Kurt?"

Her voice echoes from room to room, the house empty.

Penny, alone.

She sits on the floor in the front hallway, in a rectangle of sun, mail tucked beneath her legs. Catalogs, letters. An architecture magazine. A missing-child postcard. *Have You Seen Rusty Wells?* The postcard lists Rusty Wells's height and weight, which seems dumb since it's probably the same for every missing child ever: four feet, sixty pounds.

Your boyfriend's kind of a tool, Rusty Wells says.

"He's not my boyfriend."

Oh, okay. Keep telling yourself that.

"What do you know?"

Not much. I'm dead. Under the wheelbarrow in that field behind the old church.

"That sucks."

Tell me about it.

"Should I call the hotline or whatever?"

Nah, they won't believe you. Psychic punk chick? Yeah, right. Hey, let's send a diver after one of her hunches, maybe dredge the lake for the source of her bullshit. Anyway, I'm not in a hurry. The pastor's daughter finds me in a few weeks while she's tripping on mushrooms.

"Wait, how old are you again?"

Can't you read? Nine. Although six when I got kidnapped.

"Was it a family member?"

Landscapers. Some shitbag filling out the crew for a day, dude with a taste for chubby white boys. Just my luck, huh?

"Do they catch him?"

Nah, he's a ghost. Long gone. It's my fault anyway. If I'd laid off of the potato chips and gone outside and burned a calorie once in a while, Luiz the Molester would have grabbed up some other kid.

"Hey, I'm really sorry."

Don't worry about it. I'm the one should be sorry for what I said about your boyfriend. Honestly? I hope it works out with you guys.

"Not much chance of that," Penny says. "He took off."

No, he didn't.

Kurt pushes open the door with an armload of groceries, goes into the kitchen, slices English muffins, heats a pan for eggs.

"You want coffee?"

Penny tries to remember how to speak. Mostly, you just have to find the first word.

Well, don't leave him hanging, Rusty Wells says.

"Sure. Thanks."

On the far wall, Jack raises a glass for a toast.

Francis, who in that picture was on the wagon, raises a banana.

It's weird how the house feels empty and bruised, but in a way somehow also clean. Scrubbed of greed and acquisition. Spartan-punk. Like what it secretly wanted to be all along.

Penny cuts the deck, turns over Three Little Capitalist Pigs.

They're naked and dirty, wearing barrels instead tuxes.

Smoking blunts instead of cigars.

It was time for a change.

Even the morose Germans believed in the liberating quality of having all your shit jacked.

They call it *renewal-shtang*.

Or something.

"This shit is so sunny-side up it's ridiculous," Kurt says, bringing her breakfast over on a tray.

All Dreams
Are Night Dreams

An Aqua-Aerial Ballet

Orchestral music thunders beneath a plastic dome lined with cherubs and frescoes. Doves fly from perch to perch, groggy with chlorine. The audience boos as I swing through the rafters, high above a stage full of clowns and nymphs and polypropylene dragons.

On cue, bassoon.

And then free fall.

I'm jerked to a halt inches above the pool's surface. The harness digs in. Piper grips my wrists. The hydraulics fire and we are reeled upward again, a dozen actors on steel wire spinning clockwise around us. Piper plays the lead, the Woman in Peril. I play Grimwald, peril incarnate. Water beads down our length, mists the cheap seats. She smiles, but I can see she no longer loves me.

"Let go," she says.

"I'll never let go," I say.

And then do.

It's in the script.

Grimwald Discovered

The producers are a husband and wife team, the Arbuckles, who arrive dressed in cowl necks and cream espadrilles, like extras from *Spartacus*. It's said they have a nose for undiscovered talent and, to a lesser extent, top-quality cocaine. Which still fails to explain how they find me in Salt Lake City, laboring in a jazz-fusion production of *The Tempest*.

"We need real artistry," Jack Arbuckle says backstage, pinching arms, inspecting teeth.

The company laughs. The Arbuckles are philistines.

"Someone with a grasp of the classics as seen through a postmodern lens."

Even if that made sense, we would never.

Jack Arbuckle lights a cigar.

"Last chance, amigos."

I step forward.

The laughter stops.

Ms. Arbuckle circles, takes my measurements. After a third orbit, she nods.

"Good. You're hired. Pack your stuff."

"Right now?" I ask.

"Yeah, friend, now. You think we're spending another night in Mormonville?"

Gasps rise from the chorus. Saints, latter day or otherwise, are well represented.

"But I need time to prep my understudy."

"Okay, you have fifteen."

"Days?"

"Minutes."

The company gathers. Trinculo clasps my shoulder. Prospero strokes his rayon beard. I know then, truly, that we are a cohort. Family. Bound by a love of the theater, through long practice and a reverence for craft.

"I'm sorry, but I cannot leave Caliban midrun."

Ms. Arbuckle uncaps a marker, writes something across my palm.

"What's this?"

"Your salary."

I slide books into a duffel bag, fold a few ratty leotards. Miranda, with whom I've spent three months sharing both a cot and a stage, eyes me dolefully.

"You said you didn't care about material things."

"I'll write."

"You said you were composing a poem cycle about us."

"It will culminate with the twin themes of distance and longing."

She grabs a towel, removes her makeup with a swipe.

Beneath is the expression I once saw on the face of a man who'd been stabbed with a pen over a game of dice.

"Were you always this much of a liar, or have you just stopped acting?"

Miranda really is lovely, a touch plump but with sad brown eyes, like something from a Bob Dylan ballad about a West Village depressive who spends most of 1963 nobly expiring of tuberculosis.

"I'll put in a good word with the Arbuckles. Perhaps you can join me later."

"Perhaps you can eat shit and die."

The rear exit is dark. I channel my character's sense of loss, his quiet regret. It's not just the money; lucre can always be had. It's not the exposure, although an audience of more than a dozen would be a welcome change. It's that I saw my reflection during morning dress, looked into eyes without direction or purpose. After all these years, just a player among other players. After all these shows, owner of nothing but a mildly Victorian bearing, the face of London's usurper class.

Even though I'm from Queens.

After midnight a panel truck arrives, *Night Dreams* painted across the side. I step into the hold, which smells like canvas and cooking oil. Huddled forms slumber along the metal floor. In the corner a bearded man notches triangles of pear, swallows them from the tip of a knife.

"You must be Grimwald."

"Who is that?"

"The villain, of course."

"I have not yet been cast."

"And yet you appear born for the role."

I put down my things.

"Who are you, the cook?"

"My name is Rhydderch."

"So take it up with your parents."

He smiles grimly.

"I play the Hero. I will also be your instructor."

Taking It in the Chassis

For three days we cross the length of mercenary Nevada, bounce over desert ruts, bodies folded and then clamshelled open again like so much empty luggage. We eat Vienna sausages, piss into thirsty sand, tarantulas and armadillo skulls crunching beneath our boots. At dusk there are often rude whispers, low voices around the fire. The company is primarily Welsh, an extended family, cousins and stepsisters and third removes. They accost the driver, demand cold sodas and rum, threaten to bundle their things with twine and slip into the moonless night, jump a crab boat back to Wrexham or Llangollen.

"You will not," Rhydderch says.

The whispers cease.

By dawn we arrive at a warehouse on the outskirts of Babylon, half the cast already ensconced with stew pots and bedrolls. Crones gather kindling. Children squeal with murderous glee. Above the campfires a neon haze looms, as rehearsals begin without delay.

For some.

The company juggles cleavers and executes tuck rolls while I am made to unload trucks.

"You have a back for acting," says a strapping Taff, who carries six boxes to my two.

"And you have a face for radio," I say, half-hoping he doesn't understand.

Jack Arbuckle finally arrives and gathers the cast. Crowbars are found, crates wedged open. Oohs greet each bolt of fabric, aahs the frightening masks. There are waterproof dresses and robes, wetsuits made to look like period costume, faux velvet and mock muslin and skeins of blood-red Nu-grosgrain. If the Arbuckles have spent a penny at all, it is on these ingenious garments.

Although mine appears to be a large rubber glove.

"Try it on," Jack Arbuckle says.

It slides easily over my left hand.

"Over your head, genius."

I unzip the side and roll it past my ears like a green condom. The nostrils are plugged, the horns inverted. It's excruciating.

"The genius doesn't fit his shit," Jack Arbuckle says. "We got anyone is 20 percent less a gangly disaster?"

"But I thought you took measurements."

Ms. Arbuckle uncaps a marker, writes something across my palm.

FUCK OFF.

I decide they can unload their own trucks. It's not too late to hitchhike back to Salt Lake, wrest Caliban from the understudy, present a sheepish but lyrical poem to Miranda.

And then a woman emerges from beneath the stage, knifes into the pool, gracefully strokes its length. She is tiny, elfin. Her hair has no color, as if it wouldn't deign to be blond. She is like an advertisement for silk pajamas, a castle on Lake Como, someone else's decidedly better life.

"No, please. I can make this work. Just give me a moment."

"Fine, Shakespeare. You got sixty."

"It will not require an hour."

"Seconds."

Costumers yank. Seamstresses flit. I spin upstage, fangs bared, channel the pain of ill-designed latex and a newly compressed spine.

Come to me now, oh fire of my loins, and I will stretch your canvas, paint you a masterpiece of pleasure and sweet suffering!

Hey, I didn't write it.

Ms. Arbuckle claps and twirls.

Some of the other players join in.

"Now *that's* a Grimwald," Jack Arbuckle says, knuckling the scalp of a passing gaffer. "Can this guy do Totally Feral, or what?"

Piper breaks the surface, sloshes water across my toes.

"Who *are* you?" I whisper.

"The Woman in Peril, of course."

"You mean I am to play your opposite?"

"I guess so, yo."

As she turns and swims away, a man in a purple robe grips my shoulder.

"The lizard would do well to be less inflamed, for she is also Rhydderch's wife."

Three-Sixty-Five of Rehearsal Crammed into Seven

Ten hours a day in the pool and then a final walk-through at night, Jack Arbuckle's voice a constant stab.

"Fifty percent more erotic! Sixty percent more wanton!"

Nymphs frolic harder. Swordsmen cross weaponry. Ladies-in-waiting lie in costume, ready to be taken in the shallows.

"Grimwald! Eighty percent more evil! Ninety percent more bend-overish!"

It is not easy to balance lust with a piteous mewl.

Especially since it is my role to seduce Piper underwater.

And then hold her there.

Forever.

"Release the Night's Guard!"

Players drop from the rafters around us, tethered by wrist and ankle, swing in ovals and figure eights. If the sequence is even slightly off, they tend to collide, spears and wings and golden helmets splashing into the pool.

"Wind it up again!"

Guy-wires snap. Harnesses break. Bruises rise like dark flora.

In the midst of this madness I am expected to act. But Rhydderch is always there, with his enormous jeweled codpiece, quietly suggesting, calmly teaching, appallingly decent. Rhydderch is always by my side, whispering instructions, brandishing his sword, gripping my arm in the throes of choreographed violence that is really closer to a form of love.

"Lean away," he repeats, as we dangle in one another's arms, going over the handholds as Piper floats beneath us.

Winking up at me.

"Do you see now, Grimwald? In this position your weight must shift. Here and here, or it will not work. Here and here, or I will fall."

Oedipus Suspended, Prometheus Trussed

It's forty-eight hours from open. Rehearsals run long, verge on chaos. Scenes are cut. And then added. And then cut again. Players grumble, machinate.

There's talk of a strike.

Jack Arbuckle smiles, nods, hires a security firm, wheat-faced Pinkertons suddenly posted at every corner.

We are almost caught twice.

Once behind random tapestry and the other a rubber spear pyramid, forced to hunker next to Rhydderch's trailer out in the dusty lot.

"This is so *swag*," Piper whispers, hand jammed into my costume. "You feelin me, Boo?"

I am. And smelling her, too, like a light rain on the outskirts of Cardiff.

"Grimwald!" Jack Arbuckle yells. "Where is my goddamned lizard?"

"I have to go."

Piper pulls me closer.

"I hate this show. These Arbuckles. Vegas eats the dick. Perhaps we should escape to New York via Greyhound bus."

I picture us back in Queens, busking. Stacks of dirty nickels. A puppet theater.

"But Friday is opening night."

"YOLO, Boo."

"Please translate."

"Quit being such a puss." She grips me painfully. "Also, Rhydderch isn't my husband. He's my father."

Tympani rolls boom across the water.

"You can't be serious."

Piper kneels down and claws at the dirt, unearths a small wooden trunk, heavily padlocked, then retches into her hand, where a brass key gleams in a tiny slick of bile. Inside the box are many strange items, like children's teeth and links of vertebrae, like raven's claws and baggies of marmot dust. It's breathtakingly odd, in a way that could make an otherwise fully employed and relatively sated person long once more for the barren flats of Utah. But I am not superstitious. I know she's playing a role. I'd seen it happen with actors before, when eccentricity becomes a drug, when they lose themselves in caricature because they barely had a self to begin with.

"So you are a hobbyist witch?"

"Nah, that's just the movies."

She removes a figurine, eyeless and ancient. Possibly the totem of a people who once worshipped the feet of a people who once worshipped trees. It also appears to double as a fertility candle, since she strikes a match and lights the thick hawser's wick that protrudes from its genitals.

"Is it my imagination or is that utterly terrifying?"

"Can you shut your pie hole for a sec, Boo?"

Piper draws a chalk star around the totem, places fresh giblets along its ordinal points, and then exposes her neck.

"Bite me."

For some reason, I do.

"Harder."

My incisors puncture the skin. The candle extinguishes itself. An unearthly howl whisks across the desert floor. She stands and wipes blood from my lips, then uses it to inscribe a word into the trailer's siding:

NUR!

It could definitely be some sort of benediction.

A term of devotion in Pagan Welsh.

Or, spelled backward, it could also say,

RUN!

They Whisper of a Production Cursed

The next morning Rhydderch comes down with a fungus. An archipelago of blotches that span his chest and neck, raw and red, flaky at the edges. He walks slowly, as if having been drained or sucked dry, a shock of hair gone silver, aged twenty years overnight.

I watch him limp to the coping, gaze sadly at his reflection in the black water.

"What's wrong?"

"Nothing, my friend."

"It definitely looks like something."

"It's true that none among us can escape the Sorrows for long."

I find Piper behind the producer's box, yukking away with a muscular sound tech.

"The giblets?"

"Obvs."

"But what about the show?"

"What about it?"

"It's opening night. We can't perform without Rhydderch."

"So totally the point."

"Don't you at least want to see if the production is any good?"

"No."

"What about the other players?"

"Play yourself and you pay yourself."

"I'm sorry, but you must reverse the spell."

Her smile mirrors the ghastly face of the totem.

"Sorry, Pipes. *Should*. Probably should reverse it."

She turns on one heel.

"You are seriously starting to work my last nerve, yo."

Two Hours

"What's wrong with my Hero?" Jack Arbuckle yells at the final walk-through. "He looks like a moldy Dalmatian."

Ms. Arbuckle takes scrapings of Rhydderch with a butter knife, runs them through a CDC app on her Moto X.

"Unknown?" Jack Arbuckle says, swiping through the results. "How can there be a strain of clap left on the planet that's *unknown*?"

The company huddles and whispers, concludes the opening is cursed, the sores a retribution due us all from something dark and unappeasable, but most likely a combination of national immigration policy and uncashable checks.

Rhydderch spreads his arms, soothes in his native tongue. He insists he is fine, that rumors are rumors, that evil will ultimately be vanquished. He wraps the sores in a moss poultice, dons his codpiece and helmet, bids everyone to gather, as is custom, behind the curtains.

We peek as one through the brocaded split.

"The good news is we have a full house," Jack Arbuckle

says, as the crowd files in and takes their seats. A church group. A softball team. Older couples in shorts and sandals. Children sticky with icing. Breaded moms, portly dads, the entire front row fanning away their boredom with keno tickets.

"The bad news is we have a full house," Jack Arbuckle says.

A Review in the Laughlin Entertainer

Trust me friends, this splashy production is all wet. Does Marco Polo roll a pair of snake eyes? You bet. The daring young man on his flying trapeze drowns in a sea of lousy acting and pure cheese. Why waste your hard-earned slot points? At fifty bucks a ducat this reporter can think of much better ways of getting soaked. If I wanted to watch a princess going through the motions, I'd have stayed home with the wife. Sorry, gamblers, "Night Dreams" is a poxy two hours even Siegfried wouldn't wish on Roy. This humble reporter declares it a crap out to be avoided at all costs.

Fusarium, Ustilago, Cochliobolus

During the night Rhydderch's fungus breaks the neck barrier, eats into his cheeks and hairline. There isn't enough makeup in the world to disguise it. An ambulance comes but the paramedics refuse to touch him. A team in hazmat suits follows, finally taking him away in a large Mylar balloon.

"Oh my God, with this show already," Jack Arbuckle says. "I might as well just hand out twenties on the Strip."

"Grimwald could take over," Piper says. "For the Hero."

"I do know all the lines," I admit, force myself not to slowly run a finger along Rhydderch's gilded breastplate.

"Great idea," Jack Arbuckle says. "Arm the lizard."

Ms. Arbuckle kicks a prop, which means the show is closed for the weekend. They disappear into the producer's box to strategize.

"Let's celebrate," Piper says. "Let's go get crunked up."

We cab over to an Arthurian-themed motel, the lobby full of men with folded newspapers, caps pulled low, obsessively rechecking the line on the Lakers and Jets.

"Business or pleasure?" the clerk asks.

"Boot knocking, fool," Piper says.

We pass a bottle of Hennessy, spend the afternoon watching cartoons. For dinner Piper makes a Welsh specialty on the hot plate, something called *teisen lap*, which tastes exactly like it sounds. Afterward she showers, comes out in a cheap robe, snuggles deep into my armpit.

Maybe it's the lack of chlorine-resistant makeup, or harsh bedside light, but it seems possible she is actually in her midforties.

Or even a hundred.

"I'm way down in the dumps, Boo. I need my man to make this night all right."

"You're just tipsy."

She strokes my cheek. "Screw *Night Dreams*, okay? It's

doomed. If they want a production to work in this town it needs to be called *Biggest Free Tits*. Or, like, *Crazy Money Rape*."

When I laugh she says, "It's so not funny."

"Sorry."

"I mean, don't I have a right to the pursuit of happiness?"

"Of course."

"To marry a billionaire and watch my domestic Mexican serve important guests raw wagyu?"

"Um."

"Can't I collect awful paintings and feel jealous of my bulimic daughters and therefore mistakenly on purpose neglect to feed my pet cheetah to death like everyone else?"

Her eyes are wet, completely sincere. It's an affect achieved only by the very best actors, those who jettison all claim on fidelity, on the foolish notion that there's anything left in this world that is truly authentic. I decide it's possible she's not even Welsh. Or a woman. She has achieved the state of being nothing at all, has become a travel brochure, a folded napkin, the last melted chunk of cocktail ice.

"This is so not how you treat descendants of royalty, yo."

"You have sovereign blood?"

"Duh," she whispers. "My grandmother was the Orchid of Wales. Her third husband was the Great Melisma. They toured the pleasure houses of golden Swansea. They lived in caravans and performed for viscounts and barons."

Or perhaps leftover mutton.

Either way, I kiss her sleepy little head, both impressed and suffused with something close to something close to love.

And then when she finally passes out, I call a cab.

Half-Truths Spoken to Powerlessness

The entire wing is under quarantine. Doctors stream by with designer glasses and steel clipboards, all of them headed somewhere very important but most likely a pastry-and-nurse-filled break room. I walk by the guards with the air of a pharmaceutical sales rep who, if questioned, will no longer hand out free samples.

Rhydderch is at the end of the hall, asleep. I cough. Then give a gentle nudge. Then pound the bedrail until he startles.

"Sorry, my friend. I must have passed out again." He sips juice from a Dixie cup. "Pain is truly a demanding mistress. On the other hand, so is Piper."

I look out the window. Clouds, forever typecast, hang ominously over the mountains.

"You knew?"

"Do you think I am blind?"

"And you're not angry?"

He leans over. "Can I tell you a secret?"

"She's actually your daughter?"

Rhydderch laughs. "No. But she is quite mad."

"A steak knife in a leotard."

"Well put. Did she show you the box?"

"Yes."

"And the routine with the word? Written in blood?"

"Apparently I should run."

He strokes his beard. "Listen, don't. Okay? I like you. And *Night Dreams* is one of the best gigs I've had in forever. Besides, there's no way I can train another Grimwald in time."

"In time for what?"

A doctor comes in. Pastry on his lip, nurse on his collar.

"Okay, big man, you're a go for release."

"Wait, he's not dying?"

The doctor laughs. "Nah. But he does need to stop taking baths in raw sewage. In my professional estimation? Starting right now."

The Catalyst, the Chlorine, the Renewal

Jack Arbuckle, orangey-tan in a crinoline suit, apologizes.

"Shit, y'all. I'm sorry."

Ms. Arbuckle gang-signs a mea culpa.

Turns out the fungus didn't come from Piper's spell, but simple greed. The pool dipped a couple thousand gallons short, and instead of paying the bill, Ms. Arbuckle bribed a tanker driver to skim from the fountains at Excalibur, the grotto at Treasure Island, topping us all off with a warm untreated slurry of hamburger wrappers and cigarette butts, bobbing diapers and spattery bird relief.

"We are now pumping fresh," Jack Arbuckle promises. "We are now using expensive Egyptian charcoal filters. Plus, for the remaining length of the run, free creams and unguents for all!"

"Screw that," Piper says. She grabs a rubber boa and sunglasses, strong-arms her way through the cast, kicks open the emergency door. "I got ninety-nine problems, and y'all are ninety-eight of them."

The door closes. The alarm goes off.

Followed by the sprinkler system.

"Do not worry," Rhydderch says. "She will return."

The cast disperses. Some into the pool, some out to the parking lot to clean pans and beat rugs.

"Return to who?" I say.

Rhydderch squeezes my arm. It hurts.

"To me she has never left."

His hair is golden again, beard full and lush.

"Can I ask you a question?"

"Of course, my friend."

"Have you two rehearsed all this before?"

The corner of his mouth raises just like Piper's, an approximation so perfect they could be related.

"It's possible, yo."

The Frescoes, the Rafters, and the Ruby-Shoe Ballet

What is a play?

An exercise in repetition.

The echoing of a parroting of a redundancy.

At least if it's done right.

Every night for a month Piper hangs there, beautiful in red.

Every night for a month I hang there, like a green rubber weed.

Audience after audience cheers, wipes mist from its collective forehead, always dimly enthralled. Again and again I dive from the rafters, extend my arms, vertebrae uncoupled with the strain of holding Piper close.

Of not letting her fall.

And then Rhydderch swoops between us, stripped to the waist, on godly wings executes the Hero's Rescue.

It is a thing of beauty. An acrobatic performance that would make even the dimmest lizard newly consider the feats of men. But sometimes, even the finest of men turn sour. Revert to form. Hang stubbornly onto a lie, or the simple structure we call the wrist, or the notion that despite all the words we've used to fool ourselves, nothing will ever again fill our lonely Grimwald hearts.

There are no truths in the heart of the reptilian soul.

"Let go," Piper whispers.

"I already have," I whisper back.

Which isn't in the script.

She falls away, splashes awkwardly.

I hit the hydraulic release.

There is nothing but Rhydderch above, black water below, the screams of tourists and children and lonely gamblers echoing in my ears.

It is, after all, my role to drag the Woman in Peril to the depths.

And hold her there, forever.

Like a true professional.

You Too Can Graduate in Three Years with a Degree in Contextual Semiotics

First, tell all your friends there's no fucking way you're going to college. Drunkenly claim Nabokov is all the education you'll ever need. Hoover up stares from girls with bongs between their legs, girls with gloss on their lips, girls going to state schools, already accepted, already pitying you. Ache for them, badly.

Refuse to shake the principal's hand during graduation. Unzip your gown, show your bare chest and silver necklace. Take off in a '76 LeMans the next day, still high from the fare-well party, the one where your friend's mother cornered you and stuck her tongue in your mouth and then everyone in the kitchen laughed and threatened to call social services.

Weave down I-95 through Jersey and Delaware. Run out of gas in Baltimore. Figure what the hell.

Find a studio with a bathtub next to the fridge. Find a job at a restaurant with all-you-can-eat ribs. Be astonished by how much better you're treated than the black busboys, who are not boys but men, who've been there untold years. Be astonished that no one even bothers to pretend or complain. Think that it's sort of like how your grandmother always loved you more than your cousin and everyone knew it, even Santa.

Don't miss Rick and Amy. Don't miss Todd. Don't miss Todd fucking around on Janet and Janet calling you after a couple wine coolers. Don't miss Dylan, who's waiting tables, don't miss Sarah who's waiting to hear from that college that makes you wait, don't miss Fitz, who's sitting on the plaid couch where he will happily wait forever.

Rue the curse of having reasonable, loving parents, how their lack of animus and neglect will forever limit you as an artist.

Volunteer to serve food to the homeless on weekends. Roll dirty soup pots across dirty parking lots. Secretly hate the hippie in charge, who bitches through his red beard and stew-dripped sandals, who yells at feral Rastas and drunken runaways for not recycling their spoons.

At the edge of the park talk to a sad-eyed Russian girl who's actually bubbly and full of light. Listen to her lecture you about Moldova and how only a moron or American wouldn't know where it was. Hold her hand even though you met twenty-two minutes ago. Be amazed how cool-weird she looks in a black bodysuit and green sunglasses. Tell her you've never really had a girlfriend even if it isn't true. Think it makes you sound sensitive even though you're an emotionless cipher who flashes glimpses of humanity only when marinated in cheap beer. Pretend that as long as you're an intellectual, the sort of guy who can identify a Kandinsky or the frenzied strains of Glenn Gould, who reads three books a week even if two are crime fiction, then it's okay.

Kiss her beneath a tree. Think even her lips seem vaguely Soviet. Keep calling her Olga, even though that's not her name. Be pleasantly surprised that she tastes like coffee but not cigarettes. Buy her lunch. Buy her dinner. Buy her flat beer that costs fifty cents a mug at a bar called Murph's filled with elderly Jamaican men. Be amazed that they don't card you, even though you're barely eighteen. Think you've made friends and forged valuable inroads between cultures by dialing up five bucks' worth of Delfonics on the jukebox.

Follow Olga home that night. Find out that home is really the office of some nonprofit that helps return Israelis to Israel. Pull a battered suitcase from behind a desk. Listen to her brush her teeth in the water fountain. Lie on a couch sagging from a thousand passport-and-visa-awaiting asses. Let her get on top. Whisper her real name, Nadezhda, over and over like a talisman.

Tell the other busboys nothing happened even though Daryl says he can "smell it plain as day," which he probably can, since the office had no shower.

See Nadezhda every night. Go to shows, to movies, to bars. Help her find an apartment. Overhear her roommates mock her accent. Refrain from calling them assholes. Don't do the dishes as a form of protest. Let in the cat that hangs out in the alley, shut it in that blond girl's room. Sit on the floor and watch Nadezhda take a nap while two different copies of *Our Bodies, Ourselves* bookend the collected Kathy Acker.

At the end of a shift get tipped out a dollar by the waitress with the ponytail pulled through her Orioles cap and decide maybe college is the thing after all. Buy a *Barron's Profiles of American Colleges*, massively alphabetized, and be bored before you're even through the As. Apply to three colleges that start with B, and also Cornell.

Get accepted to two.

Let your father pretend that's not why he started talking to you again. Decide to major in film. Let your father pretend that's not why he's no longer talking to you again.

Have hoarse and whispery conversations with Nadezhda about maybe coming too. Rub her wrist through the hole in her sweater, wipe her nose, promise no matter what to be *this* close and *this* chaste, endlessly on the other end of a phone. Vow to disprove distance as a theory, across a thousand miles feel her ghost stomach pressed nakedly against yours. Promise to exchange mad letters, inexhaustible sentences, fragments of brilliance, declarations of proclamations of edicts, a compact signed each time in blood or even deeper.

Secretly decide that you want to go alone. That there's no way you're showing up in an unexplored city, the blank canvas of a new campus, saddled with something long-term. Love her, lust for her, think the word "besotted" without laughing at yourself and still fail to deny that loving her, lusting for her, thinking the word "besotted" without laughing at yourself is a knife, a cleft into the meat of you that makes you vulnerable, that makes you want to run barefoot in the dark and sweaty heat in one direction until you are at least two atlas pages away. Or 12 percent less a melodramatic asshole.

The night before you go listen to Nadezhda cry during *Moonlighting.* Be smoochy, then resigned, then annoyed. Her messy hair. Her red, crumpled face. Say no, you're right, it's not funny. Volunteer to grab dinner, come back to find her gone. Eat all the fries on principle. Fail to produce a clever relationship analogy about empty ketchup packets. Write it on a napkin anyway. Call her four times, no answer, no answer, no answer, angry roommate. Threaten an ass kicking you could deliver but won't. Get more than a little drunk.

School. Take a slate of production classes. Quickly come to terms with what horseshit they are. Immediately accept that not a single person in the department will ever actually make a film. Immediately accept that all the professors gave up on L.A. after a few years, never did anything but unfinish screenplays and complain about traffic, moved home to teach nineteen-year-olds the rudiments of slapping together four minutes of underexposed film of a naked sophomore wearing a leather mask and call it a degree.

Switch majors. To Russian lit. After a week decide it's too grim, too Gulagy. Snag the last spot in Intro to Syntactics and Pragmatics. Start quoting Roland Barthes. Use "Saussurean" in a sentence at a party. Fail to connect with Derrida over the course of six hundred pages. Connect to Coover in a single sentence. Question a friend's signification. Vow to name your first daughter "Ferdinand." Pretend to read Wittgenstein in the caf. Wear a beret, discard it. Wear scarves, discard them. Earring in, earring out. Crib a paper on Bertrand Russell's years-long ménage à trois as it relates to sexual pragmatism in mathematical empiricism. Graduate.

Move to San Francisco, don't get hired at an anarchist bookstore, don't get hired by a video game developer, don't get hired at a magazine to do rudimentary layout, and especially don't bother to install one of the Netscape mailers that arrive on your doorstep every day, under the impression that ignoring the Internet is probably what the New York Dolls would do, a vital political statement but with 30 percent less eyeliner.

Decide chat rooms are a symbol for death. Decide cell phones are an emblem for death. Decide computers are a representation of death. Decide television is an allegory for death.

Two jobs, then a third. Bosses. Girls. That tall one with all the hair, later a Thai who likes Iggy Pop. Pin the arm back on to a suit. Go to a friend's funeral, a guy who drank too much and fell down, randomly hit his head on the cement next to the grass next to the keg. Have your boots resoled. Pick out a new car, listen to the pitch, argue about the invoice, sign the papers, drive it away from the grinning Ukrainian salesman.

Send Nadezhda the money for a bus ticket. Let her yawn, act like she's considering. Is she seeing someone? Maybe. Do they matter? Whose business is it? Plead then cajole then beg. In begging find something you didn't know was there, a willingness to be humiliated (just another modality) and also not give a shit (purely lexical and without true meaning). Listen to her say yes. Melt with *umwelt*.

A hug at the busy station. People streaming by. Clock the businessmen who roll their eyes, couples who elbow and remember when. Wait for the inevitable "Get a room!" The moron's guffaw. Say nothing when Nadezhda stiffens. Say nothing when she pretends to be busy with her suitcase, leaves your roses on a bench.

Go to tourist spots you're also seeing for the first time. Secretly think the cable car and Alcatraz are cool but pretend they're dumb. End up giving some tourist dad the finger, his crying kids. Have no answer when she asks what's wrong with you. Over dinner you can't afford, get in an argument about Dave Eggers. Order the most expensive dessert just on principle, leave it untouched. Order cheap wine, one bottle and then another, don't leave a drop.

Be yelled at while leaning against a brick wall.

Apologize. Admit you know you're damaged. Make a joke about how Black Flag has an album called *Damaged*, so maybe it's okay? Laugh at her not laughing. Mention that you're writing a novel and that's why you've been so preoccupied. Be startled by the pity in her eyes.

Have sex in the kitchen. Sort of wish you didn't. Ask why women always have to cry after. Sort of wish you hadn't.

Her on the futon, you on the couch.

In the morning, Nadezhda's partially rehearsed lecture about all the ways you've changed. Soak it in over eggs Benedict at a place called La Flora, your coffee refilled by sassy waiters who make sympathetic faces behind her back.

Drop Nadezhda off at the bus station, help load the same battered Samsonite into the hold. Aim for a rousing, theatrical good-bye for the people already in their seats, and deliver. Whisper, "I love you," in her ear, watch the people watching be surprised by her laugh.

Call a month later, be told by some guy with a voice like a flexed quad that she's not there anymore.

"Said she was bored."

"Bored?"

"Decided to move to Jerusalem."

"Jerusalem?"

Spend that winter imagining an earnest kibbutz. Working in the fields, elaborate feasts, everyone in torn fatigues and sexy skirts. Dodging Scuds and making out behind piles of organic kale, idly leafing through the Pentateuch in the hottest hours. Flirt with the idea of adopting some kind of faith—in her, in human nature, in a bearded divinity floating on a gilded cabbage leaf, a god who loves the humble and hates random masturbators, a god who deigns to bless your inevitable gentile/goy son, a boy who becomes a man who becomes a great leader that drives some tribe into the sea at the end of a cutlass, but not the Palestinians, because, frankly, they've got some legitimate complaints despite what Zeki said around the fire the other night.

Stop drinking, get a better job. Write three chapters of a roman à clef about zombie symbology, think it'd be better as a graphic novel. Wish for the nine hundredth time you could draw. Take pictures that will never be famous or hung in the Whitney. Write poems that will never be read aloud or adjudged remotely poetic. Volunteer at a pirate store that's really a front for teaching low-income kids to read. Meet other men with similar politics, meet other girls with clingy red dresses, have other complaints. Stare into a series of serious eyes, plunge between a series of unfamiliar legs, by the third date fail to be the person you could be for them if only you were different.

Lie on a recently reupholstered couch with a woman you don't love. Watch *Friends* and the commercials between *Friends* while eating rigatoni.

Become a manager, button the top one. Fire people who don't realize you're actually pretty cool it's just that someone has to enforce the rules. Get another tattoo, worse than the third. Buy an insanely expensive bike, stare at the broken lock on the sidewalk. Visit Texas, win a distance-spitting contest. Smoke PCP by mistake, feel irreparably insane for eight days, not so much on the ninth. Bury your parents within six months of each other. Argue with an uncle, shine off an aunt. Decide that no one can be told anything, that the world is a grand bargain, a fraudulent transaction, a complicity of bullshit.

Wake in the middle of the night, sure she's thinking of you. Buy a ticket, get on a plane. Spend a month with a backpack and a water bottle searching the fertile crescent for the girl no one has ever heard of, the woman no one has ever seen.

Float on your back in the Red Sea. Get tan and then brown. Drink with on-duty women, armed men, dance in small, sweaty clubs until dawn and then noon and then midnight again.

Show Nadezhda's picture around hotel lobbies, in bars, in spots where the homeless are being fed.

Tear up your visa, which expired anyway. Find an apartment, date a corporal, kill off another year. Turn thirty, something you finally have a diploma for.

Marry Rivka.

Have a child. Then another.

Push a stroller, buy ice creams, laugh with bearded dads in tiny parks, always on the lookout.

Even ten years later, as you drive Doron to school, as you sit through Gideon's violin recital, as you stand alone in a tiled hallway during intermission, close your eyes and count to three, positive you will turn around and Nadezhda will be there, at the water fountain, chin wet, smiling.

And Now Let's Have Some Fun

The Old School was packed, rows of hard wooden benches arrayed above a makeshift stage. In the center was a ring, canvas spotted and gray, ropes actually rope. Torches hung from the rafters and smoke obscured the crowd, which swayed and howled in unison, like a single gaping mouth.

Nurse stood in Primo's corner. She wore tight starched whites, a tiny skirt and heels, ignored the wolf whistles and catcalls.

"C'mon, Champ. Circle left. No, my left. That's it. Now gimme some combinations."

Primo punished the air until the Albatross's handlers led him in. There were cheers and a smattering of bird calls. The Albatross danced, cooed, vinyl wings flapping as the crowd ate it up. Bettors yelled, "Straight Win, Albatross!" (2–1) and "Da Champ Choked Out Quick" (5–2), while Mr. Fancy recorded wagers and Abe Golem stuffed cash into the canvas bag chained to his waist.

The Albatross stepped in with arms raised, absorbed the cheers like fuel. Sweat rolled from his bald head, soaked his pink leotard. His real name was Darnell. He and Primo had trained together way back, but the Albatross had gone punchy after a tough loss to Kid Spastic and couldn't really be talked to anymore. Or at least counted on to answer in anything but chirps and whistles.

The mic was lowered. Buddy Vox's golden age of radio voice boomed. "Welcome, Gentlemen, to the final bout of this evening's Spectacle. As always, there is to be *no stabbing*. Souvenir knives are just that. Souvenirs. Also, the pinching of Beverage Girls is forbidden to those who have not paid this month's Fondling Dues. Ask your nearest server how to get your account in good standing. This is your last chance to wager. Why go home underbet? Also, why not have a steak? Contact your nearest server and tell her 'Buddy Vox likes it *so* rare' and you'll get an extra 10 percent off. Once again, any stabbing will result in a lifetime ban from the Spectacle. And now let's have some fun!"

Ding.

The Albatross charged with a combination of kicks and elbows. Primo dodged him easily. The crowd screamed or groaned, depending. Side bets, like "Next Left to Land" (3–1), "Slips and Almost Falls But Not Quite" (7–2), or "Da Champ

Strokes Out, Cannot Be Revived" (40–1) got heavy play. The Albatross caught Primo with a few solid kicks, tried to reopen the gash on his cheek. Primo targeted the ribs. They traded jabs up to the bell.

"Breathe," Nurse urged, squeezed a sponge over his head. Her breath smelled impossibly clean, as always, like cilantro and lime. She rubbed Primo's shoulders and Vaselined his ears while he leaned back, rested against her chest.

"Who's ahead?"

"I call it even. So stop effin' around."

"Tryin' to be smart. Guy's a butcher."

"And you a pussy. Don't mean you got to act like one."

Ding.

The Albatross fluttered over. Primo dropped his guard, baited the Albatross into a wild uppercut before shoving him against the ropes and tearing off his left wing. It sailed into the crowd. A group of brokers went crazy, holding up a ticket for "Both Wings Torn" (46–1) until Mr. Fancy explained that "Yes, that sure was a savvy bet, and congratulations! Really. It's just that the fighter in question is, as you can see, still Partially Winged." The suits bitched and whined and poked the air with their cigars until Abe Golem loomed over and stood behind them.

"Pay attention!" Nurse yelled, as the Albatross worked free and tried a spinning backhand. Primo ducked and drove his heel into the larger man's kneecap, shattering it. The Albatross fell, tried to rise, stayed down.

"Winner . . . *Da Champeen!*" Buddy Vox warbled, over a wash of boos and spilled paregoric.

Doc Nob twirled his mustache. "Will you just look at this piece of shit?"

The Albatross lay on an exam table, blubbering quietly. Primo sat at his locker wearing a towel, too tired to move. Doc Nob broke a hypo off in the Albatross's thigh, manipulating the kneecap for a while before declaring the whole enchilada medically pointless.

"You concur?"

Nurse stuck out her tongue.

Nob dropped three pills onto it.

"You concur?"

She nodded, signed the form.

Nob pressed the intercom. "Can we get a clean up already?"

"Not a clean up," Primo said.

"None of your business, Champ."

An orderly who looked like Veronica Lake in desperate need of a shave kicked open the door, pointed at the Albatross.

"This mess?"

"That mess."

She wheeled the exam table out into the alley and then threw the bolt. Dogs began to bark and snarl.

"Anything else?"

"Go get Mr. Fancy."

The orderly blew Doc Nob a kiss, skipped back up the stairs.

"She new?" Nurse asked.

"Of course."

"Where you find them at?"

"I dunno. Bars. Under bridges." He turned to Primo. "How's Gina?"

Primo gingerly pulled on slacks. The answer was *dying*.

"Same, I guess."

Nob rooted around his Gladstone for a prescription bottle.

"Give her six reds and ten purples. Before breakfast. No milk."

"Thanks. What do I owe you?"

"Nothing."

"Nothing?"

"Yet."

Mr. Fancy walked in, held up a check. Doc Nob snatched it and disappeared. Nurse picked up a robe with a slit in the back to accommodate wings, dropped it in the trash.

"Yeah, listen, it's too bad about the Albatross," Mr. Fancy said, chewing a cocktail straw. He wore a Mao jacket and round glasses and looked almost exactly like John Lennon in pictures where John Lennon is so high he looks almost exactly like a small Chinese man. Behind Fancy, as always, was Abe Golem. "But the beak? The fluttering and cheeping already? Ho-hum."

"Yeah," croaked Abe Golem. "Ho-hum."

"Also, on the news front? I've got some bad news."

Abe Golem nodded. "News."

"The thing is? I can't use you again this month, Champeen. That's the thing. That's it for you. This month."

Primo pawed at his duffel. He needed a little over twenty thousand more for the big plan. He and Gina would fly back to Tokyo. Already had the tickets and a down payment on an apartment. Top floor. A doorman with brushes on his shoulders. Picture windows and pay cable. Also, there was a doctor. Akashimi. Did experimental shit with a laser or something.

"That's not gonna work. I got bills."

"Yeah, well, what *I* got is a busload of Brazilians. Steaming north this minute. Actually, cannibals. One of my scouts found them. Way out in the jungle. Guy almost didn't come back, too busy scouting to notice he'd make a nice brisket."

"Brisket," said Abe Golem.

"Anyway, I figure I'll have them go at it for a while, learn the ropes. Who knows how long to cancel each other out? A day? A month? Cannibals? Shit. Anyway, you're on hiatus, Champeen. The crowd's getting bored with your shtick. Blah, blah, *was at one time considered pound-for-pound the greatest in places they measure greatness by pounds*, blah. It's like, 'So What' (1–1) at this point."

Abe Golem opened the canvas bag at his waist. Mr. Fancy reached in and counted out three thousand dollars. "So here's your cut. Say by August or so? Maybe I'll have something then. I'll send Abe over to let you know."

Primo shook his head. "Not him. Not at the store."

"Okay, okay, I'll send Vox. How's business, anyhow?"

Yesterday they'd had two customers. The day before none at all.

"Booming."

Mr. Fancy lit a long, thin cigarette, and then immediately put it out.

"Well, stay in shape, Champ. A smart man's always ready when his time comes."

PRIMO DROVE HOME with the windows up and a pipe wrench across his lap. Plastic smoldered on every corner. Torn dresses and flat wallets and tiny Crocs littered the street. At night, teenagers took over the recycling plants and held raves. They laughed at people who still used the word *rave*. They cut up magazines and smashed bottles and sang Boy George. They fired their weapons and fondled their concubines and goaded each other with jagged tuna lids until dawn.

Gina was still awake, on the couch in her favorite lipstick, watching television. *Therapy Fred's Upswing Hour.* A bald man in a cheap suit listened patiently as women complained about being left or cheated on or just plain ugly. He had a soothing voice and a southern accent that promised Reasonably Sustained Remedy. Once Therapy Fred found your Road to Remedy, he smiled through his mustache and showed the way. Or went to commercial, depending. To the crying woman on stage he said, "Kick your husband to the curb, sweetheart, and then put on some mascara and go find someone with the life skills to treat you anywhere from 18 to 22 percent better!"

The crowd stood and cheered.

"Hey, babe."

"Daddy?"

"No, it's me. Primo."

"Where's Daddy?"

"Dead."

"For a long time?"

"Yeah, babe. Twenty years."

"Oh."

He kissed her temple. She held his hand and stroked it. Her wedding ring gleamed dully, just a setting, the diamond long since disappeared.

Primo was working late the night Gina guzzled the floor wax. He found her in the hallway, in nothing but a bra, green foam bubbling out her mouth like a science fair volcano. He raced her to the hospital, where they pumped her stomach. After six months she'd recovered enough for therapy. There were speech classes (Pin cushion. Say it. *Say* it. Pin. *Say* it. Cushion. Pin cushion. Good.) and life classes (Do we give out our credit card number over the phone? No. Do we leave dirt in the toilet without flushing? No. Do we swallow most of a bottle of floor wax? Probably no.) and coping classes (Sometimes it's okay to scream. Good. Great! Like an animal. *Grrr.* Fantastic! But the scratching? No. *Ouch.* No.).

"Can I have a Popsicle?"

"Sorry, babe. It's too late for dessert."

"Then can I have a story?"

Over the television was a picture of Young Primo in a gold frame. It was taken in Tokyo. His arms were raised, in the middle of the ring, the night he beat Bulldog Funches for the belt. It was like two lives ago. Primo stared. The man in the picture stared back, fit, delirious, barely a mark on him. He'd been way too much for Funches that night. The bulbs flashed and reporters clamored and Gina sat in the front row, newly ascendant on the modeling circuit and cashing insane checks, beautiful, serene, wearing the most expensive dress in all of Japan.

"I only got one story, hon. But it's a good one."

"Okay," she said happily.

Primo picked his wife up and carried her into the bedroom. When her bathrobe fell open, he forced himself not to look.

BUDDY VOX STROLLED down the aisle, ran a finger along shelf after shelf of Mack Threes and SnagWire and Flux Drives shaped like tiny assholes that came preloaded with the latest Ha Ha Insert It Here app.

"Nice place you got, Champ."

"Yeah," Primo said.

Vox licked his fingers and smoothed his eyebrows, tiny yellow teeth matched by a tiny nose and ears and eyes, all congregated too tightly in the center of his face. "Buddy Vox believes in your small businessman, your family farmer. Do I say that because I have a parent or grandparent who was one? An extended relation who filled those shoes? No, I don't. Still, you have my full support."

A group of teenagers stood by the electronics shelf, too thin, too silent, too interested in the new Thumb Rocket X, which allowed you to text without texting. Primo kept an eye on them while he swept the floor.

"Anyway, the Gobbler is 20 and 0," Buddy Vox said, leaning on a display case in his white tux. "Crazy Brazilian, no one can beat him. Can't touch him. Too fast. And those pointy teeth? Scary. Oh, man, *fumble*. Is Buddy Vox scared? No way. But maybe. I have to admit. A little."

"Watch the glass," Primo said, wiping Vox's prints with his cuff.

"Dang, my bad."

"It's fine."

"No, for real, let me make it up to you."

Vox stuck out his chin, pointed at the point.

"Send me into orbit. Go ahead and ring my cowbell, Champ."

"You were saying? About the Brazilian?"

"Right. Do the crowds love this Gobbler? It's blood, blood, blood. Not on my shoes. I'm careful. But everyone else's? Oh, boy." Vox looked down at his gleaming wing-tips, just to make sure. "The Gobbler's already gone through his entire tribe, plus half our roster. The Sandman and Ed Abattoir are finished. Der Berliner and Lardy Gaga too. Even Mistah Ka-Ra-Tay is done. Did the Gobbler bite a hole the

size of a grapefruit in Anarchy Punk's back? Yup. Did he sink
his molars into Rick Windex? Well, let's just say that guy'll
never streak a pane again."

There was a muffled explosion down the street. The teenagers left in a group. Primo walked over to the shelf, where
SCREW DAD'S ACQUISITION CULTURE! and BY ANY MEANS
NECESSARY BUT STILL WITHIN REASON! were scratched into
the plastic. All the Thumb Rocket Xs were gone.

"Oh, and Chiming Wind?" Vox said. "You should have
seen him try a takedown defense with that hippie spirit crap.
The mentalism? The incense? Did it work? No."

"He dead?"

"Maybe. But it's like, what's dead even mean anymore?"

Primo nodded. Chiming Wind had been a pretty good
guy. They'd had a couple of drinks once.

"Shit has gotten drastic. For real. So Mr. Fancy sent me to
ask you back, Champeen. Hell, they sent me to beg you back.
Am I a pimp? No. Didn't all of Buddy Vox's music teachers say
Buddy Vox had the best voice they'd ever heard? Yes. Didn't
they swear Buddy Vox would win various competitions and
awards and top prizes? You bet. But here I am anyway, on my
hands and knees."

"Bottom line."

"Fancy's offering triple fee to start. Plus a cut of all Non-
Bite wagers."

"Ten percent."

Vox looked both ways, leaned over. He smelled like a rag
soaked in bitters.

"I'm authorized to go up to twenty, so you got it. Right off the bat. Would I dicker with you, Champ? No. Would Mr. Fancy be pleased if he knew I was spreading my legs like some loose ring girl? No. But still. Here we are. At 20 percent."

"Venue?"

"We're out at the Old Barn now. So much blood at the Old School you couldn't mop it anymore. The orderlies were threatening strike."

A wiry kid with a goatee poked his head in the door.

"You sell ammo?"

"No."

"How about Cutty?"

"No."

The door closed.

"When?"

"Friday," Vox said. "But you watch yourself, Champeen. I never announced anything like this Gobbler. Money's money, sure, but I was you? I might just retire."

"Tell Fancy I'll be there."

"You got it, Champ."

"Now go."

"You got it, Champ."

Primo turned to ring up a woman buying the Peggy Fleminator, a vacuum you wore like skates, one on each foot. You flicked the switch and glided around the house, sucking up all the dog hair and lost buttons and clots of dust that made each waking moment such a singular misery.

"Does this really work?" the woman asked.

"Yes ma'am," he answered, shoving the Fleminator into a large paper bag.

AT DAWN PRIMO strapped on ankle weights and jogged through the woods behind Safetown. He did six fast miles and then doubled back by the Old College, a group of buildings burned to the ground, bare timbers and scorched brick. The bleachers were still intact though, and he ran up and down the steps, three at a time.

"What, you got a new trainer? Don't want me no more?"

Nurse sat in the grass, on a car seat burned to the springs. Her hair was cropped close, purple mascara and little white cap, all honey-thighed in a tight starched skirt. She looked like a Vietnamese hit girl. Someone who would make you cry. Someone who would cut your back with a razor, just because razors were made for cutting.

"Getting in a little road work. I need you to tell me left, right, left?"

"You gonna fight this Gobbler, you do. And a whole lot else besides."

Primo got down and knocked off crunches. Nurse tapped a rhythm, *two-two-three*, *three-two-three*, with a stick. After a while she said, "Told Fancy I'm done. No more corner woman. No more cut woman. No more Miss Two Percent."

"Good." Primo grunted, touching elbows to knees. "Past time."

"Yeah, well, maybe it's past time you do the same."

Primo picked up the pace. His stomach burned. "Can't (huff). You know why, I know why (grunt). So what're we even talking about?"

Nurse yanked at weeds that poked through the skeleton of the seat. She stuck one in her mouth, grimaced, spat it out. "Yeah, well. This little runt is bad news. I been watching. I seen him eat his way through half a dozen guys like they were buttered toast."

Primo lay back and caught his breath. He rubbed his eyes, yellow spirals dancing beneath the lids.

"So?"

"So even if you stepped from some time machine, all twenty-one and hungry again? All *I'm on top of the world, Ma!* I still don't know if that guy beats this guy."

"Gonna have to. Too late to back out. There is no back. There is no out."

Nurse ran purple fingernails the length of her nylons.

"How's your old lady?"

Primo hadn't actually been working late the night Gina swallowed the Floor Fiesta. He'd been training with Nurse. Training up to the hilt in Nurse. Had been for months. Gina knew or she didn't. Cared or she didn't. Never said a word. Either way, he was a piece of shit and nothing could ever change that fact. No amount of being hit would ever be enough.

"The same."

"Uh-huh. And you?"

"Need another week to make weight."

"Not talking about training."

Primo stood, watched the silent overpass, wondered how long until it got the joke and just toppled over.

"Listen, you could come with us maybe. Get your own place, settle in."

"Japan? Fuck that. You don't read the news? Whole island glows."

"Can't be any worse than here."

"Wanna bet?"

"Are you crying?"

Nurse wiped her face. "Nah. Allergies."

They stood close, breathing hard. She pressed her mouth to his. His hands left trails of sweat, began to pull at her blouse before wrenching away.

"Fuck."

"That's the idea, genius."

A series of booms cascaded up the valley. Primo ducked, but Nurse didn't even flinch. There was heavy machine gun fire and then a much larger explosion that silenced it all.

"Let me ask you something."

Nurse exhaled, breath sterile, eyes glassy, higher than any kite would ever go. Primo was tempted to climb on up there with her, rest for a while.

"What?"

"You know any good cut men? I mean, now that you told Mr. Fancy you're through. Anyone else you could recommend to stand at my back while I fight this Gobbler?"

She half-smiled. "Cut *woman*."

"Right."

"Someone fast and talented? With a wealth of experience? Maybe a touch exotic?"

"An empress in white."

Nurse took his hand and held the swollen knuckles, kissed them one at a time.

"Yeah, I might could scare someone up."

ON FRIDAY THE Old Barn was raucous. Every seat full, suits crammed into aisles and fire exits, four to a step, all of them screaming, nearly unhinged. Primo punched the air while bettors lined up to put money on "Immediately Raked with Incisors," even at a prohibitive (2–5). Beverage Girls stepped like flamingos, no space for their stiletto heels. Men pushed and shoved in front of Doc Nob's Olde Tyme Injection Booth, waiting to be pricked.

Buddy Vox, in a pink cummerbund, reached for the mic.

"And now, friends . . . in the main event . . . the Jewel of the Amazon . . . the Prince of Peridontia . . . the Little Stomach That Could . . . pound-for-pound the most savage fighter to ever grace a Spectacle ring . . . *the Gobbler!*"

A prolonged roar shook the rafters, as an orderly led the Gobbler in on all fours. He strained at the end of a steel chain, giggled and spit and swung his head from side to side. Buddy Vox held the ropes apart, but the Gobbler leapt over them and landed in the center of the ring, letting out a wail that sounded pre-Columbian. Prelanguage. The crowd went crazy. Money flew. Mr. Fancy snapped his pencil, trying to get down all the bets. "Calf Gnawed Like Hoagie" (2–1) was getting lots of play, as well as "Da Champ Cries Like a Little Bitch" (3–1). The sole nonbite wager in his favor, Primo noticed, was "Da Champ Pulls Off Some Tom Hanks Miracle" (100–1), which hadn't gotten a sniff.

So much for his 20 percent.

Buddy Vox finished an extralong announcement speech. There'd been two stabbings at the last Spectacle and no one was happy about it. Souvenir knife sales were temporarily halted. "Please, *no stabbing*. Really. Are we kidding? No. Why does everyone think we're kidding? We're not. So take a second to sheath yourself. Also, go ahead and order a porterhouse. Tell your nearest server, 'Buddy Vox likes it *so* damn rare' for an extra 6 percent off. And now let's have some fun!"

The crowd noise was almost painful. Primo leaned against the ropes, trying to concentrate.

"You keep movin'," Nurse whispered from behind. "Move, move, move." She put her lips against his earlobe. "He insane quick. Can't stand and trade. Gotta get on your horse. Stay still, you're done. *Move*."

The Gobbler clawed the canvas, crouching and spitting. He was tiny. Maybe five-two but one solid muscle, like a bar of soap. His skin was a glistening teak, covered with tattoos and feathers, a stick through his nose and hair plastered to his skull with orange mud.

"You ready, Champ?" Vox asked.

Primo nodded.

"You ready Gobbler?"

The Gobbler grinned like a piranha.

"To *ze* victor, *ze* spoils!" Buddy Vox intoned.

THE DAY AFTER the Bulldog Funches bout, Primo and Gina walked down a path lined with cherry blossoms, other couples milling around an ornate wooden shrine. It was cool, a mild Pacific sun casting long shadows over crushed gravel and elaborate shrubbery. There were banners hung on wooden poles, simple drawings of tigers and bears, austere symbols in black ink. Gina asked an old man what they meant. He smiled broadly and bowed.

"Man don't speak English," Primo said.

"Neither do you," Gina answered.

They watched him shuffle away in cloth sandals. The sun began to set. Two children played with paper birds, repeatedly folded, that seemed to hover in the air. No one here knew what Primo had done to Funches. No one here needed to.

As if reading his mind, Gina said, "I don't want you to fight. Ever again."

"Why?"

"It's too dangerous."

He took off the enormous sunglasses that hid the swelling around his eyes.

"Then I won't."

"You don't mean it."

"Try me."

Gina threw her arms around his neck. Primo inhaled her scent, coconut and linen and a trace of sweat. She wore a kimono they'd bought at the Honshu market, tiny clerks showing how to wrap and tie. He lost his hands in the folds. It was such a cliché, but they'd met in eighth grade, by a locker, and immediately he knew. That quiet smile and checked skirt. She claimed not to be interested, said he was too big, too coarse, didn't raise his hand enough. She was a virgin, her father a hard-ass with a racing form in his back pocket and a silver cross dangling from the rearview. Primo told her at a party he could wait. He'd train, live at the gym. She could pretend as long as she needed to, but one day he would lean over and brush his lips along her bare shoulder like it was the most natural thing in the world.

And he was right.

THE ENTIRE FIRST round Primo *ran*, barely managing to dodge the Gobbler, each pass a gnashing of teeth that caught only air, loud and wet and savage, missing by inches. The Gobbler's movements were electric, tiny hops, cartwheels and back flips, all the while those teeth grinding like something with pistons and gears, *chomp chomp chomp*, like something built to extract marrow.

FOR A YEAR Primo and Gina shared a tiny apartment, one room and a kitchen. It didn't matter. His gloves and trophies and equipment sat in a box in the closet. She hung tapestries, created walls, gave the illusion of space. Primo drank wine for the first time in his life. Gina read poetry and danced to scratchy Nat Cole records. They lay in bed while candles burned, fit seamlessly against one another.

IN THE SECOND round, the Gobbler began to find his range, quick little nips, shot Primo's guard, scampered under his left, a series of bites and welts, all of them bleeding. The only punches Primo managed fell on the Gobbler's back or shoulders, the tiny bastard too quick, somehow able to anticipate a blow and contort his least vulnerable part in its path. Primo backpedaled, giving up damage for breath, punching for space, not even trying to land.

TWO DAYS AFTER Primo found out Gina was pregnant, he bought the store. She got bigger and needed help getting off the sofa. Primo cooked terrible dinners and bid on new inventory and outfitted the car with a baby seat, top of the line. In the final trimester they went to the doctor's. There was a test, just routine, then a complication, which wasn't.

AT THE END of the third round Mr. Fancy climbed the ropes. Abe Golem held him by the ribcage until he and Primo were face to face. "What in fuck're you doing, Champeen? I'm taking a beating here. "Twenty Percent Blood Loss" is paying *three-to-one*! "Gobbler Flosses with Ankle" is ten-to-one and has already paid twice. You can't let this degenerate beat you. I got no one left. Next week he's gonna have to fight himself!"

"Fights himself and every bet wins," Abe Golem intoned.

"Exactly. It's like you're sleepwalking, Champ. Jab and stick, jab and stick. Christ. What did you train all those years for, huh? Or did that turd Funches take a dive?"

Abe Golem put Mr. Fancy down and they shuffled off to take more bets.

"Don't pay no attention to him," Nurse whispered, kneading Primo's shoulders. "Just fight your fight, got me? Fight your fight."

THE DOCTOR UNTIED his mask and strapped on his sympathy, explained the unexplainable in a rush of jargon and honed concern. Gina was in a room with four other women, all of them sedated. Primo went across the street to a bar and had six whiskeys before getting into a fight with an enormous red-faced Pole, losing badly, only half on purpose.

THE BELL RANG. The Gobbler leapt from his corner and sank his teeth into Primo's arm. Primo threw an uppercut that missed, a right that missed, a kick that missed. The Gobbler gnawed some leg before slipping back out of range.

"Jesus, Throw in the Towel Already" lowered to (3–1).

Wanna thrive, gotta come da fuck alive! the Albatross used to say, back when he still talked.

Even had it tattooed across his chest.

For once, the crazy bird was right.

Primo dropped all pretense of technique. He charged, forced the Gobbler into a corner, and threw a roundhouse lifted straight from the movies. All windup and shoulder. It caught the Gobbler flush in the mouth. It was a better punch than he ever hit Funches with. It was a better punch than he ever hit *anyone* with. Primo's knuckles ached inside their wraps. The crowd fell silent. The Gobbler woozed back and grabbed the ropes with one hand, reached into his mouth with the other. For a comical second he rooted around, eventually pulled out a tiny razor tooth. He held it up, whimpering, while it gleamed like a diamond under the lights.

Nurse whistled.

Mr. Fancy and Abe Golem stopped collecting bets.

Primo cocked his left.

And then the Gobbler went Completely Insane.

He screamed and frothed and showered the crowd with bloody spit. He pulled out his nose stick, tossed it over his shoulder, and charged. It was a jabbering, bug-eyed attack. Primo countered without thought.

They met in the air, like a pair of rams.

And bounced off one another, falling to the canvas.

"Oh, my god," moaned a stock analyst in the front row, jumping up and down. He'd put ten grand on "Fighter Ditches Rationality as Working Concept" (163–1) and wanted to collect. So did all his pals. Mr. Fancy tried to explain how insanity was relative and wondered if the gentleman was indeed a trained psychoanalyst and therefore capable of making such a determination. "No? What is insane, really, anyhow? Are not our great artists and philosophers still wrestling with that question? And so, unfortunately, your bet is No Good." The analyst argued. Abe Golem loomed. The entire section came to the guy's defense. The bet was good. It had to be paid. A chant began. Mr. Fancy saw what was coming and changed his verdict. "Fine. Everything is fine. Really." He tried to open the canvas bag, but Abe Golem fumbled with the chain and by then it was too late. A riot began. Someone in gabardine stabbed Doc Nob. Mr. Fancy disappeared beneath a lofted chair. From the top row, the thin, reedy voice of an Internet entrepreneur requested help. Abe Golem grabbed a lawyer by the collarbone and swung him like a three iron, trying to clear a path toward his boss.

Primo, dazed, forced himself to stand. The Gobbler began to slink forward on all fours. Primo warded him off with a series of kicks.

"What're we doin', Nurse?"

He glanced back, but Nurse was no longer in the corner. The stool was knocked over and some idiot was wearing the spit bucket on his head.

The Gobbler inched closer.

Primo tried to gauge the odds of making the same side door that Buddy Vox had just slipped through. A path opened where a section of crowd had their backs turned, surrounding a trio of Beverage Girls making a brave stand, shoes in either hand, razor heels swung in wide arcs, carving suit.

Primo saw himself vault the ropes. He'd find Nurse, grab her by the collar, sprint into the gap.

It was a long shot. It was the only shot.

He pivoted, flexed, took two steps.

And then slipped in his own blood.

"Da Champ Eats Shit" (16–1).

The gap closed.

The Beverage Girls disappeared under a wave of French cuffs.

Primo managed to get on one knee as the Gobbler sprang, landed squarely on his back. The weight drove Primo flat. A rib cracked. The crowd roared, a vibration welling through the canvas and into his chest. Primo, pinned, thought about Gina. She would be at home, on the couch. If Therapy Fred had a remedy for her now it would be *Next time, marry a winner.*

Sirens wailed. A fire started, smoke billowing toward the rafters. The sprinkler system went off, a deluge of rusty water, like rain in the Amazon. Nurse was lying in the aisle, on her side, staring at nothing.

"Show's over," Primo rasped, unable to move. "Nada mas."

No answer.

"Comprende?"

The Gobbler's teeth clicked and gnashed. A powerful stink wafted from his gums. Rotted lamb and scorched metal. Ruin.

"Yeah, I comprende."

"Wait, you speak English?"

The Gobbler leaned forward, whispered in Primo's ear.

"I'm from Jersey, asshole."

"Not Brazil."

"No, papi."

Primo exhaled. There was still a chance. He could offer the guy money, maybe tip him to Nob's stash.

"Thank Christ. They said you were a cannibal."

The Gobbler giggled. His fingernails dug in.

"At least they got one thing right."

Primo tried to reach back and get a grip, but his gloves were wet and the thumb was useless. Arcs of pain, like camera flashes, exploded in his head. The Ring Girls were a blur and Abe Golem's shoes were a blur. Someone screamed, and then someone else joined in, hitting the same desperate note. Rain gently pattered. Smoke settled in the corners. Primo pressed his cheek against the canvas, inhaling the smell of rubber and sweat, while the Gobbler ate parts of him he couldn't afford to lose.

Tiffany Marzano's Got a Record

The warehouse takes up an entire city block. St. Cloud is the manager. He used to be infantry but got kicked out for asking *and* telling. Now he's an artist, wears a snake around his neck. Sometimes you can see the bulge of a mouse beneath the coils. He waits on the dock while Jake and Tiffany Marzano back another load of donations in.

Workers circle, push and shove, make claims on the haul. Everyone at the warehouse is allowed to steal one thing. But it can only be one thing, and you have to be consistent or St. Cloud decides you're greedy and it's a pink slip. A skinny blond does furs. The dock guys handle stereos. There's someone for comic books, screen prints, silverware. A guy in a trucker cap prices Italian shoes, ships them to New York in bulk.

St. Cloud does toasters.

Jake hops out of the truck and presents him with a vintage top loader, chrome and Bakelite, looks like it fell off Sputnik in 1962. St. Cloud mounts the toasters in galleries with names like *Char-O* and *Count Van Der Slice*. When one doesn't measure up it goes on the scrap pile. All around the warehouse are different piles: sweaters, coffee makers, Les Baxter albums, sofa cushions, boom boxes, reading glasses.

No one steals reading glasses. It's a wide-open niche.

THEY HEAD OUT on another run. The truck smells of Tiffany Marzano, so Jake smells of Tiffany Marzano. Even with the windows down. There's a sleeping bag in the hold. Cans of chili roll with every turn. When Jake asks Tiffany Marzano if she's living in back, the truck veers into a motel courtyard, lurches to a stop.

"Why, you gonna tell?"

"No."

"You sure?"

Jake is. He would never.

"Listen, I did eleven months behind a misunderstanding," she says, all shoulders and brown skin, a shark's tooth around her neck on a tight leather strap. On weekends Tiffany Marzano plays three sets as El Vez, the butchest Presley this side of Tucson. "Now I'm on a registry. No one will rent me a room."

"What kind of misunderstanding?"

"Does it matter?"

Probably not. Jake needs the job not the drama, been clean almost eleven months.

"It's cool. Let's roll."

Tiffany Marzano rams it into gear. Time is money. They get paid by the load. The Truck of the Dead grinds up hills, down hills, spews resignation and exhaust into every last corner of San Francisco.

It's 1992, the middle of a health crisis.

A citywide emergency.

Or maybe the CIA gave everyone AIDS on purpose.

Either way, it's also Friday, and Jake needs to cash his check at the deli on Valencia. If he doesn't get there before five, Luz, the owner, runs out of cash. She's a tiny Salvadoran with a flowered smock and faded blue angels on her neck. She'll smile at Jake, but not at Tiffany Marzano.

"Tiff is alright," Jake whispers. "Give her a chance."

Luz rolls her eyes, tosses in two *mios* for every *dios*, recounts the money.

WAREHOUSE FUCKING is rampant.

There's a group of men, a couple women, like a club. A press gang. Going at it in utility closets and dimly lit storage rooms. Behind vast piles of donations, pyramids of broken microwaves and mismatched shoes, curls of ejaculate across dusty cement that might as well be raw plutonium.

Jake does not fuck.

It's been over a year.

Just the thought of being touched, by anyone or anything, fills him with an elastic dread. Even a shower seems too intimate. He tends to scrub over the sink with a wet cloth, keep his shirt on, eyes shut.

Sex and death are the same thing, all the neon stickers say so.

Being high is also death, but at least comes in euphoric increments.

Since Jake has nothing to show for his twenties but a handful of nods, some insipid lyrics, and endocarditis, he figures it's probably best not to judge. Even though the Warehouse Fuckers circled him at first, made insinuations, played with his hair.

Jake told Luna, the dispatcher, who said, "Try being less hot."

Jake told St. Cloud, the manager, who said, "Gotta learn to deal, girlfriend."

Jake told Tiffany Marzano, who threw a Warehouse Fucker off the loading dock and then stomped on another's lunch.

Flat banana, flat banana, flat hummus wrap.

The orbiting stopped.

PROCEEDS FROM THE sale of donations go to charities with a variety of acronyms and intentions. Some deliver vegan meals, run triple-blind trials, or give away rubbers wrapped like gold doubloons. Another trains Dobermans for the sickly to pet bedside.

At least that's what the pamphlet says.

Jake takes a picture of the mole above Tiffany Marzano's lip as Luna's voice cuts through the radio.

"Home base. Over. Jake? You there?"

Luna is also Jake's roommate.

"I know you're listening. Grab the handset already."

Jake rarely grabs the handset.

"You're late. The client has complained twice. St. Cloud is righteously pissed. Kindly move ass. Over."

"We need a direction," Tiffany Marzano says.

Jake's map is marked with red stars, like crime scenes. Longitude and latitude might as well be Mandarin and Cantonese. Before he was hired, St. Cloud quizzed him with an atlas. Jake guessed six times, got five right. He also had to fill out a questionnaire. *Are you familiar with local topography? Do you have an opinion on sexual orientation?* Also, *what's it like being a vampire?* Jake realizes he may have hallucinated the last one. He's been tested sixteen times, clean sixteen times, still positive the virus is secretly eating into his brain, occluding his thoughts. Who's to say that he isn't already dead, discovered cold and blue on a hardwood floor, just another tedious overdose waiting to rise at dusk?

Tiffany Marzano snaps her fingers. "Right or left?"

The truth is they're lost. Cars behind them lay on the horn. Jake shuts his eyes, prays to whatever god will have him and a few who won't.

A stack of boxes suddenly appears.

"Over there. The driveway."

Tiffany Marzano double-clutches, backs in. A client stands in front of his garage, next to an array of Dead Boyfriend items, stuff he can't wait to get rid of, never wants to let go.

"Our condolences," Jake says, and begins to triage. Junk first, wedged into the crush zone by the stove. Valuables last, up front and wrapped with packing foam. There's a brand new Nikon in a leather case. A bag of socks. A sconce and an ottoman. A vintage bowling shirt that has KEVIN sewn over the breast pocket.

The client looks like he's about to cry. Jake would give the client a hug, except then the client might notice Jake's complete lack of body heat or pulse. Also, all the way home Tiffany Marzano would make Jake recite Tiffany Marzano's List of All the Things Caring Will Get You.

"Where do I sign?" the client asks.

"No papers," Tiffany Marzano says, although there are. Practically a novella's worth. But names trigger reminiscences. Reminiscences become Kleenex. Kleenex is the difference between completing three or six hauls.

Tiffany Marzano is an instrument of change, not a grief counselor.

Almost no one asks for the papers twice.

ACROSS THE KITCHEN walls are photographs by Jake, tacked into plaster, chronological. One a day for a year, all of Tiffany Marzano. Always in profile, always behind the wheel. Framed by stoplights and street corners, buildings and people, the time-lapse orange that is San Francisco trivial in the face of her stare.

"Welcome home, sweetie," Luna says, sprawled on the couch, blond and pale and 80 percent ass. It's a popular look. A series of sleepover dates wait in towels outside the bathroom on Saturday mornings. There aren't many repeaters. Luna likes to dangle them at arm's length, feel their scales, toss them back. She prefers an ongoing scientific sample. Once there was a guy named Jordan for almost a month and then she had to delete the data and start over again.

"So did you ask her?"

Every day at noon Tiffany Marzano takes the truck. For exactly one hour. Doesn't say where or why. For weeks Luna has been bothering Jake about it. She plays in a band called Mr. Teriyaki. Their landlord's name is also Mr. Teriyaki. He owns a company that makes rubber vaginas. The different models all have names. Perky Pam. Moan Jett. Deep Erin. They come in a velvet pouch. In exchange for rent, every four months Luna drives a load to St. Louis. This time she wants to pocket the U-Haul cash, use the Truck of the Dead instead.

"I'm not asking anyone anything."

Luna frowns. "I think Tiff's got a stash out in the avenues. I bet she's hoarding dining room sets and vintage toasters."

"No way."

Everyone knows Tiffany Marzano doesn't steal, which makes them nervous. The fear of investigation lingers over the warehouse like scorched hair, visions of men from corporate busting through the doors with tracking numbers and donation printouts, dock guys who turned so many stereos into so much powder taken away in cuffs.

"Yeah, but if we tell St. Cloud, he'll suspend her and then I'll be back in a week and no one will even notice the truck was gone."

"What if she gets fired?"

"Nah," Luna says.

Jake picks up the remote, which is broken. He finds an Eveready in a drawer filled with dimes and birthday candles. The 49ers blink from the screen. There's an interception. One of the linebackers punches the goalpost like a boxer. The crowd cheers, slaps five. Jake longs to be so high that the entire stadium laughs as he floats past, hovers six feet above their cowlicks and bald spots and dry umbrellas.

It's not the discipline, he thinks.

Being sober? It's the colossal boredom.

THE PHONE SITS on a table in the hallway. Jake's mother's ring is distinctive, all the way from Tampa, still hasn't figured the time change. Jake gets out of bed, still dark, dream erection, picks up the receiver.

"Hello?"

"Your father is out in the yard again. He won't come in."

Jake's father has dementia, thinks he's storming Normandy with Red Buttons. Which is good, because if he remembered who he used to be, his sodden bastard of a résumé, he'd shit himself more than he already does.

"Leave him alone, Mom. You know the drill."

"Also, the counter is full of envelopes. From school. They all say IMPORTANT. In red."

Jake owes $23,500 in student loans. He is the recipient of a degree in photography from a criminally uninteresting midwestern college. His advisor was a woman who thumbed from Vermont to sixties Alabama and took iconic pictures of marches and water hoses, of police dogs and burning court-houses. A tough act to follow. There was pretty much nothing for Jake to shoot on campus except his friends doing drugs, the shadows cast by another leafless tree, that girl with out-rageous pubic hair.

Besides, now everything's digital. It's like he spent four years learning how to use a cotton gin.

"What you should do, Mom, is throw that mail away."

"All of it?"

"All of it."

"Not important?"

"Not important."

Luna cracks the door to her room, puts a finger to her lips. Some guy lies on the futon behind her, snoring.

"Pierre?" Jake guesses. "Adam? Jonah? Billy?"

Luna giggles, gives Jake the finger, shuts the door.

"Who's there? Who're you talking to?"

"Put some crackers and a glass of milk on the porch, Ma. After a while he'll wander back in."

IT'S NOON. Luna stands next to Jake on the loading dock. Beneath them three homeless negotiate over something inscrutable, but probably vodka. Luna takes Jake's hand as the Truck of the Dead pulls from the lot with a chirp.

"C'mon, let's get something to eat."

There's a burrito place around the corner. The register boy has straight hair and glasses. His front tooth is set in a little frame of gold. Jake and the register boy grin at one another three lunches a week. Jake has been test-driving his Spanish, as well as current events. For instance, *pico de gallo* means "tip of the rooster." For instance, the 1988 Mexican general election was stolen away from Cuauhtémoc Cárdenas Solórzano by the PRI, a conservative party that has been in power for nearly a hundred years.

"Well, now we have no choice," Luna says, peels foil from a burrito the size of a toddler. "I told St. Cloud all about Tiff's stash. He says we need proof. Or, you know, something proof-ish. So tomorrow at lunch we're following the truck."

"Follow it how?"

"I sort of have a car."

Luna has never had a car. There has never been any mention of a car. Jake has carried her amp dozens of blocks to Mr. Teriyaki shows, never the hint of a ride.

"Since when?"

"Yesterday. I traded a first-edition Bukowski."

Luna does books, brings home a trash bag full every day, sells them to the secondhand place on Cesar Chavez. The owner is a former sleepover. Jake does cameras. He badly wanted not to steal, and for a while didn't, but he could feel the Warehouse Fuckers resenting him, sort of like *Serpico* except with better facial hair. Mostly, though, not stealing was Tiffany Marzano's thing and Jake didn't want people to think he was copying Tiffany Marzano.

"I'm not going."

"Sure you are."

"It's isn't right."

Luna retrieves a pinto bean from her collar, eats it.

"Sure it is."

Jake raises his new Nikon. He wants to take a picture of the register boy but is out of film, so he aims at Luna instead. She sucks in her cheeks, continues to look exactly like Luna.

The flash bangs and rolls back across the room, again and again.

THE CAR IS a blue Accord. There are stickers with clever sayings on the dashboard, sticky black rectangles where less clever ones have been peeled away. Luna has been excited all morning, working on the story she'll tell later: Tiffany Marzano robs *banks*, Tiffany Marzano fucks *sailors*, Tiffany Marzano is a hit man for a *Shanghai triad*.

"Oh, wait," she says. "My sunglasses."

While Luna's inside, Jake lets the air out of the Accord's front tire and then walks across the lot. The hold is mostly empty. There's a rolled up carpet, a chest of drawers, and a tall wooden packing crate. The crate is half full of pants. Dead people's pants. Jake gets in, covers himself just as Tiffany Marzano starts the engine.

The Truck of the Dead crosses town, moves gracefully

around Sevilles idling in the street, young men leaning in passenger-side windows. Tiffany Marzano makes turns with the butt of one palm, rarely touches the brake, whistles "Viva Las Vegas" in and out of lanes. She is in utter control of all speeds, angles, vectors. She is the Sugar Ray Robinson of driving.

The usual icons glide by, the orange bridge, the phallic tower, the island jail. Jake's back begins to hurt. The denim smells wheaty with grime. Finally the truck stops and Tiffany Marzano gets out. They're parked on the industrial side of the bay, near a performance arts school. The water is a shabby blue. Trawlers chug in circles. Windsurfers lean into the gusts.

Jake watches Tiffany Marzano buy a hot dog from a cart, eat it in two bites, pick a bench. Students stream past her, around her, laugh and yell and slap one another's backpacks. Some wear uniforms, some wear costumes. A Tybalt and a Mercutio spar with wooden swords.

Jake climbs out, walks over.

"You were in the truck, uh?"

He nods, takes two pictures.

"Thought I saw you in the rearview. Figured maybe I should open the back door, let that crate slide out into traffic."

"You would never. Also, Luna told St. Cloud."

"Told him what?"

"I dunno. What you're up to."

"What am I up to?"

"I guess this."

"Your girlfriend is a cunt."

"She's not my girlfriend."

"Your roommate is a cunt."

"Yeah. I'm sort of moving out."

Tiffany Marzano smiles as a little girl runs over, white sweater and pigtails. Jake takes two pictures, brackets the aperture, takes one more. Tiffany Marzano leans over and removes the Nikon from his hand, snaps the lens clean from the body, lobs it at a pigeon that barely deigns to move. The little girl laughs. She has a mole near her lip, ringlets of black hair set against a white dress.

"What's your name?" Jake asks.

"Summer."

Tiffany Marzano and Summer talk for a while, hug, tell secrets. Locker doors slam. Tennis balls pong in spurts. Finally, a bell rings and Summer jumps up, runs back toward the school.

"So yeah, I took her down south for a couple weeks. Just to the beach. Matinees and fried clams. A little pink motel. Her father has custody, but I brought her back. Was always going to. Still, we roll up and asshole's got a lawyer plus half the force waiting in the driveway."

Jake tries to imagine Husband Marzano. Wraparounds and a goatee? College wrestler with a flattop, still lifts twice a week? Or maybe a mouse with round glasses, washes up after dinner without being asked.

"I thought you were queer."

"So now I got lunch visitation. Also, a record."

Another parent comes over and shakes Tiffany Marzano's hand. There's talk of a fundraiser, T-shirts for the soccer team. They bump knuckles and the woman goes away.

"This place must really cost," Jake says.

The bell rings one more time. The grounds are quiet. Vendors lower their umbrellas, begin to leave. Tiffany Marzano is wearing chef's pants, the kind with a drawstring and little blue checks. There's a tan ring of skin between the hem and her boot. A gold anklet with an emerald charm hangs in the gap.

Jake has seen it before. At a client's. Triaged it into the hold himself.

Tiffany Marzano yawns, stretches, steals after all.

"Every night I park the truck on a different street. People walk by, have their conversations, their arguments, no idea I'm there. It's snug. I got candles. I got books and wine and a sleeping bag. The hold makes this ticking sound as it cools, sort of like music. And then when the sun comes up, it expands again."

"Sounds nice."

"Yeah, but they were gonna find out, take the keys away eventually."

"I could talk to St. Cloud."

"You could, huh?"

"I think he likes me."

Tiffany Marzano turns. Her face is different from the front, prettier.

"At first I thought you were dumb. Then stoned. Now? Who knows?"

"I'm a vampire," Jake says, adopting a thick Hungarian accent. "I may not have mentioned before."

"Nope, I'd have remembered that."

"Yes, I remember thees place back ven eet was just rocks and grass. Ven there were only horses and pale stable boys and ze hint of plague as it rose from mounds of burning garbage."

"Sounds nice."

"Yeah, but they were gonna find out, stake me in the heart eventually."

Tiffany Marzano laughs, holds out her wrist. "Well drink up, Vlad. We got three more hauls to do."

Jake takes her hand, warm and rough, presses it to his cheek.

Flesh degrades but antique Turkish rugs persevere. Memories fade while busts of Maria Callas callously seek new homes.

There will always be more donations, they will never stop.

There will always be too many cars and not enough streets, traffic all the way to the pandemic.

The sun will set, and then it will be night.

The moon will rise again on the decadent carcass of San Francisco, and by then Jake will be very, very high.

Comedy Hour

I am the point guard, best player, and team captain.

Which means we suck.

At least until Makarov transfers to West Boylston.

"We've got a new teammate," Coach Grout says, with four days of gray stubble and a belly like he's smuggling hams. "All the way from Ukraine or whatever. Let's make him feel at home, okay Bolts?"

There are a few smirks. A couple comments. The dude is tall but way skinny. With Coke-bottle glasses and Russian sneakers that don't even have a name. No swoosh, no nothing. Hair that would be mod if it were intentional, all feet and hands, looks like he's about twelve.

"SCRIMMAGE!" Coach yells.

I bring the ball up, right away brick a three. Makarov

skies for the rebound, makes a move that leaves Washington duct-taped to the floor, dribble, dribble, dunk.

"Wow," says Poltroni, a chubby Italian with hair on his neck.

"Wow," says Xavier, lean and springy and accurate within twelve feet.

Coach Grout just chews his whistle.

I trot over and inbound to Washington. But Washington isn't there. Makarov is. Pale, unblinking. Like some Siberian deer hunted way past extinction. And then *twitch*, he steals the pass, spins, dunks off my head. Everyone on the bench laughs. All six people in the bleachers laugh. My brother, Steve, who's watching from the doorway, laughs.

"Still only counts for two points," I say.

"There are twos and there are *twos*," Poltroni says.

Coach diagrams an elaborate play, X defeating O. Makarov sort of sign-languages that in this case, we actually want O to win. Coach erases furiously. He redraws and O comes out on top. Everyone nods.

I look over and Steve's gone.

Then Coach blows his whistle, kicking off another hour of nonstop Makarov highlights.

THAT WAS TWO months ago. Now we're 14–0, the West Boylston Bolts in first place, Makarov averaging 38 a game. We stomp Warren G. Harding by 20. We crush Hamilton Poly and Winthorp Remedial with ease. The Fitchburg game, Coach has the scrubs in halfway through the second quarter.

"SCRUBS!" he yells, and even their parents chuckle. Someone starts a chant: "WE SHOUT FOR GROUT!" A dozen fans join in and the gym echoes *out out out*. The Fitchburg kids are scared. Their coach is sweating and their parents are silent and Makarov keeps flashing his grin at the end of the bench. Our scrubs score maybe twice in the second half and we still win by a dozen.

I BLOW OFF my last class. My brother is waiting in the parking lot.

"Need a ride?"

He's got cool shades and dangly hair and one enormous arm resting against the side of his vintage truck. Of course it's *vintage*. Why can't it just be a truck? Of course it's *dangly*, why can't it just be hair? I sling my duffel into the flatbed, where it clonks against tools and scrap metal. It's scrap because Steve works. There are tools because he can fix things. Like, for instance, your broken heart. Just ask half the cheerleaders in town.

Or their moms.

People watch with envy as I jump in.

"Belt up," Steve says.

I put my foot on the dash.

"Foot off the dash," Steve says.

I leave it there.

The truck backfires like a cannon as we squeal by a line of kids walking to the gym. They stare and point. My brother is still a legend at West Boylston. First for sports, but that fades.

Then for girls, but they eventually graduate. Now it's mainly for being big and cool and not rubbing it in everyone's face all the time.

"Want to check out Comedy Hour?"

"You know it."

There's a dry cleaners at the top of the hill that overlooks school. Steve eases around back, in the shade of a padlocked Dumpster. It hides the truck but gives us a sniper's view of oncoming traffic below.

I spark the joint, blow a plume in his face.

"Where you get this dirt weed anyhow?"

"Quiet, it's starting."

Once the final bell rings, cars pour out of school and grind up the hill, where they disappear into an ancient train tunnel. It's a vestige from the pioneer days, cut straight through wet granite. Somehow being beneath all that rock lulls people into thinking they're safe, unwatched. For a hundred yards of darkness they revert to their lizard brain, can't help but get a little weird.

And then each car emerges right below us into a shock of bright sun.

Like a paparazzi flash, a startled portrait, *snap!*

The dullest are captured up to the third knuckle, excavating sinus. Others sing or dance, pop and lock, eyes pinned like bats swooping down on a grape. Their faces are manic or slack, stoned or terrified, netted fish and Chilean miners. Dudes grip their tools in lonely boredom. Girls drop the pose, lipstick smeared. There's chubby transfers and balding teachers, band geeks and burnouts, mathletes and athletes, the beautiful and the ignored, all framed behind a windshield, all unwitting and beautifully innocent, *snap!*

We weep with laughter, rock the cab, punch each other's shoulders in disbelief.

"Dude! No way. Check it. Check him out! Look. Look at her! Oh, dude! Oh, DUDE!"

Comedy Hour makes me want to give every student a hug and a snack, each teacher a pat on the back, makes me like my worst enemy so much more. In fact, it's probably the best show in the history of television.

Except maybe the part when Angie Bangs drives by in her mom's Jaguar. She always emerges unscathed, fine and composed and not the least bit hilarious. Partly because the truly beautiful are almost never compromised by anything, bright light or tunnels or random opinions, and partly because I've been in love with her since eighth grade, which everyone in school but Steve apparently knew about, a fact that became obvious after he hooked up with her at a party a few weekends ago.

I found out after her best friend bragged in the caf, people leaning over the table to hear the details, spilling each others' milk, going, "Whoa! Way to go, Angie *Bangs.*"

I could have gotten pissed. Called Steve out, clenched my fists, let the tears and snot rise. Thrown a few punches he'd easily dodge. Or even worse, let them land. But what's the point? He'd just sit there with his trust-me eyes and go, "Are you sure?" and I'd be like "Yes!" and he'd go "Wait, who again?" and I'd be like "Angie, motherfucker!" and then he'd be all puzzled and caring and quietly skeptical, "Man, if you say so."

We pull back onto Route 4, leave a patch, cut off a Camaro that would normally give us the finger and scream, except the driver recognizes Steve's truck and makes with a friendly *bip bip* instead.

"So what's with you coming to practice all of a sudden?" I ask.

"What about it?"

"I keep seeing you out of the corner of my eye like, wait, Dad's busted again?"

Steve laughs, since we both know there's bail money in a salisbury steak box in the freezer.

"I wouldn't come for that. Also, you guys don't suck nearly as hard as usual."

"Yeah, something's definitely changed. None of us can quite put a finger on it."

We roar around a slow Honda, yank back into our lane with inches to spare.

"So who's the new guy?"

"Just a transfer."

"From where?"

"I dunno." I say. "Albania. Romania. Buttfuckistan. Seriously, though. How come you keep coming?"

Steve reaches over with his Popeye arm and puts me in a headlock, runs a knuckle across my scalp while steering with his knees.

"Why, there some law says I can't watch my little bro and his pals play with their balls?"

THAT FRIDAY THE stands are packed to the gills. The parking lot's full and there's a big line waiting for the john. Girls stand around in circles, squealing. Boys stand around in leather jackets that don't fit. Everyone wants Makarov's autograph: *Sign my math book! Sign my purse!* He just grins like he doesn't understand. You wish to exchange beads for the island of Manhattan? The government has declared this whole area irradiated? He shakes his head, runs through layup drills while scouts wait with stopwatches and hotdogs and pads full of little calculations. Under the stanchion are six photographers, flash flash flash, shots of Makarov running, dribbling, swooping down on the ball like a thirsty vampire. West Boylston hasn't had a winning season in ten years. The Bolts are a standing joke, *Hey Bolts, Go Screw!*

Not anymore.

The game starts and Makarov immediately goes behind the back to a wide-open Xavier. Poltroni drives and kicks, sets me up for easy jumpers. Coach is wearing a suit with no visible egg stains. Even Washington seems to have a pulse. There's love in the air and we win by 36. It could have been 60.

IN THE SHOWER I'm like, "Dude, how's your English coming?"

"English good," he says, sniffs the shampoo like it's some exotic bouquet. Or maybe food.

"Don't eat that," I say.

He doesn't answer.

I'm like, "Where do you live, anyhow?"

"Live good," he says, and then towels off, zips into the same tracksuit he's been wearing pretty much since the first day, some too-shiny Russian brand doesn't even have a name, no swoosh, no nothing.

AFTER PRACTICE, WE pile into Washington's Nova. It's a '77 with a stock .351. A very fast car. At least it would be, if Washington didn't drive like my grandma.

"Open it up!" Poltroni says.

"Punch it!" Xavier says.

"Mmm-hmmph you," Washington tells them, scratching the Afro above his sad-dog face. He signals early for a left, eases around a corner, careful not to go over 300 RPM's in third.

Xavier pounds the seat, "Team!"

Poltroni pounds the seat, "Bolts!"

"Watch the mmm-hmmphing upholstery," Washington says.

The car finally creeps into the lot of West Boylston Rim and Radial, where Steve works. Their motto is *Done in under an hour, or it's free,* which isn't true. Washington finds a spot, a good two feet of space on either side. He pulls out, readjusts, backs in again.

"There's your brother," says Poltroni, pointing into the shop. He leans over and toots the horn, nice and respectful, *bip bip*. Steve rolls out from under a Lexus. He's got a jump-suit on, no sleeves. The wrestler biceps. Grease on chin. He looks like an ad for beer that claims to be colder than other beer, the kind secretaries tape above their computers. It's hard to believe we're related.

"It's hard to believe you're related," Xavier says.

Steve liked working at West Boylston Rim and Radial so much he dropped out senior year, quit the football team even though he was being recruited for division II. No one could understand why and Steve wouldn't say, so they made up their own reasons, decided it was some sort of principled stance. Steve giving the finger to the man. Steve refusing to become part of the machine. But I knew that if he graduated he'd have to *graduate*. By staying in West Boylston and keeping his mouth shut, he let the world create its own myth. Not to mention believe it.

"No more school," he told Dad, in his quiet-for-Dad voice. "From now on I'm a working man."

We were standing in the kitchen. Dad pulled his jammies tighter.

"Fine. Then from now on you're a rent-paying man, too."

Steve fished in his pocket, sprinkled the counter with twenties. "Let me know when that runs out."

Dad turned to me. "Well?"

I bussed tables. At Ribeye Rob's. Most of my tips were in quarters. It barely kept me in jocks and slices. "Can't. I'm on the team."

He gave me a look, flattened the bills on the stove. "What team?"

Dad doesn't leave the house much. He doesn't shave except when he does, and then you remember he has a chin.

"Little man's pretty good," Steve said, cracking a beer. "Or wait, am I thinking of someone else?"

Dad laughed.

"Dude's got a lot of moxie though. You can't teach moxie."

"Can't teach anything," Dad said. "Nothing to know."

Which isn't true. There's just all things you don't understand, or want to admit to yourself.

For instance, how yesterday morning I opened the door to my brother's room without knocking.

Like I always did, late for practice and out of socks.

And then almost shit myself. Right there on the orange rug.

I could hear Coach's voice, *SPRINT!*

But didn't move.

At least not until Makarov woke up. All pale and lanky. Content. He winked and smiled. Stretched and yawned and snuggled a little closer under my brother's arm. The blanket was pulled around them, radio on low, Dire Straits blending perfectly with Steve's quiet snore.

Then I did sprint.

All the way to school, no breakfast, nothing. The gym was empty. I sat in my underwear and hyperventilated for about an hour. Then I destroyed some scrub's locker with a piece of pipe from the boiler room. After a while, Coach came out of his office and looked at the mangled door, confused. He put his hand on my shoulder.

"Problem?"

"No, Coach."

He scratched his ass and then scratched his neck and then scratched his nose.

"Well, keep up the good work."

"Yessir."

After a while the guys showed up. They yelled and threw stuff and grab-assed all around me.

The scrub stared at his ruined locker and didn't say a word.

Makarov ran through practice and didn't say a word.

I took a long shower and dripped a trail of soap all the way to algebra. When the teacher called on me to solve for $y = q - 2$, I just sat there and didn't say a word.

"Hey bro," steve says, walking out of the shop and leaning against the Nova. He holds out his hand to slap five. Washington and Poltroni and Xavier stand behind me, hands in pockets, silent with the usual awe.

"We'll take an eighth," I say.

Steve flashes his badass squint.

"That all? None of you superstars got jobs?"

Poltroni lets out a greedy laugh, until he realizes he's the only one.

Steve pulls a Ziploc from his bib. "Well, don't smoke it all at once."

I give him two twenties. "Well, don't spend it all on one dude."

The guys stare at me in alarm, then back at my brother. Who looks like he's about to stuff me into a grease barrel and roll it out into the bay.

"Drive careful," he says, slow-jumpsuits back to work.

"What the mmm-hmmph that about?" Washington asks.

Xavier assesses the baggie with his thumbs, "*Nice.*"

Poltroni eyeballs it, holding it up to the light, "*Nice.*"

"Can we go now?" I ask.

On friday we're down a dozen at halftime. Winslow Homer Tech has a guy six-eleven and plays a tight zone. I've missed my first three shots. Makarov has his usual twenty-eight, but their big man is scoring over Washington at will.

In the locker room Coach is pissed, tears us a new ass.

"PLAY!"

We all nod.

"HARDER!"

In the hallway a scout leans against the wall wearing a forties newsman hat and expensive sneakers.

"Hey, kid," he says, waves me over. I figure he wants to ask about Makarov, but instead he goes, "You're a good little player. You thinking about college?"

"I guess."

"You heard of Southern Community?"

"No."

"Yeah, well, we're a small program." He opens a snack cake and drops the wrapper on the floor. "Downstate. I think maybe we could use a smart player like you."

"For real?"

"Depends how bad you want it."

Up until that second it didn't seem possible, so I never bothered to want it at all.

"We talking scholarship?"

He clicks his stopwatch. On. Off. On. He licks his fingers. "Nah. You pay your own way first year, see what happens. You stick, maybe we have something to talk about over the summer."

"And if I don't stick?"

He shrugs, tongue dark with Ring Ding. "Worse comes to worse, you got a year's worth of Algebra II under your belt."

I could bus a million ribs and still not swing tuition.

"You'll think of a way," he says, reading my mind. "Smart kid like you."

When I get back to the bench, Washington pulls me aside, "What that mmm-hmmpher want?"

"Guy thinks I got skills."

Washington laughs. "No, really. What he want?"

MAKAROV GOES NUTS in the third quarter, dropping bombs from the wing, floating toward the rim, lefty, righty, backpedal, fade away. He's unbelievable. The crowd's in a frenzy, stomping feet, punching air. It's like being inside a snare drum. Makarov steals the ball, goes between the legs. Makarov takes a pass, sinks a rainbow jumper. Makarov beats his man, two-handed facial.

The crowd starts a chant, "WHY POUT? WE'VE GOT GROUT!"

And then, "BOLTS! BOLTS! BOLTS! BOLTS! BOLTS!"

And then, "MA-KA-ROV! GETS-US-OFF!"

They go ahead, we go ahead. With four minutes left, Washington fouls out. We're forced to put Xavier and a scrub on their big man. It's like handing out free points. I make them pay with a runner in the lane. Their guy rams one down Xavier's throat. Neither team can land the big punch.

"SCORE!" Coach yells.

There's thirty seconds left and we're down one. The crowd's too hoarse to scream anymore, switches to a strange low-rumble moan. I dribble right, dribble left, holding for the last shot.

"HOLD FOR THE LAST SHOT!" Coach yells.

When Makarov finally breaks open, I'll toss over the ball and watch him throw it in. Everyone in the place knows that's the script. Even the Winslow Homer guys seem resigned. The freckly kid guarding me confirms it with his sad eyes.

Ten seconds.

Six.

I spin around Freckle, top of the key. Makarov comes off Xavier's screen, wide open.

Four seconds.

I'm about to execute a perfect chest-pass when I spot Steve in the front row. The bleachers are packed, a thousand people standing as one. But Steve's not standing. He's leaning back, like a king. His face is pinched and greedy. His hair dangles and his boots gleam and there is no place, no box or hole or drawer in the world big enough to hide the fact that he's staring at Makarov's ass.

So NOW WE'RE 16–1 and everybody's pissed. Coach makes me do extra push-ups and Washington takes off after school, not asking do I want a ride. I have to hitchhike to Ribeye Rob's, half an hour late.

"You're late," says the manager, pointing to his rated-for-300-meters dive watch. His tie pin is shaped like a diamond spatula.

"I know," I say. "Sorry."

"Sorry doesn't bus tables. Go police your section."

I put on my apron and hit the floor. At least a dozen tables need setups. The salad bar could use a refill of everything but sprouts. There's a waterless party of eight and a slick of spilled prawns by the register.

It takes about an hour, but I'm almost caught up when some old guy leans over his steak, "Way to go."

"Excuse me?"

"A thirty footer? You?"

So, yeah, I didn't pass the ball.

What I did instead was launch a thirty-*two* footer. Man, it felt good. High arc, perfect follow through. Spinning so slow I could see the air hole every time around.

Coach screamed, "NO!"

The crowd screamed, "NO!"

Even Makarov shelved the grin, his face blank, astonished. The entire gym inhaled as the ball nubbed back iron and spun around the rim, then let out a collective *wuff* as it rolled off and fell to the floor.

AT MIDNIGHT I toss trash into the Dumpster and empty rib bones into the grinder and scrape grease off my loafers with a paring knife. Georgie the cook is smoking a cigarette on the loading dock, all tattoos and grill burns, a big silver cross hanging around his neck. Georgie played some high school ball himself. I know that because three times a shift he says, *Y'know, I played some high school ball myself.*

"You effed up, dude."

"You think?"

"Dude from thirty feet!" he says, in excited-announcer voice, "Dude decides he's Allen effin Iverson!"

I pull up a milk crate and we puff together for a while. The lot is slightly melted and smells like dirty ketchup. You can hear crickets and birds and other things trying to live in the tall grass between the median. You can hear truck brakes whining and AM radios and the long satisfying whoosh of cars careening off the exit. It's the opposite of Comedy Hour. There is no tunnel, no reveal. From darkness into more darkness.

"Don't sweat it, dude," Georgie says, and twists his cigarette, saving the short for later.

"Ready to punch out?" I ask.

He nods, points to a line of ants carrying rib fat through a crack in the wall.

"Now that's teamwork."

So WE WIN our next two games, nothing special, ahead by 20 and the scrubs in at halftime. The ship rights itself. Coach starts letting me off with only a hundred push-ups and Washington's giving me rides again, but something feels different. Like going through the motions. Like going through the motions backward.

Steve stops coming to games, won't answer his phone.

Dad hasn't come out of his room for a week.

Even Makarov isn't smiling anymore. He's missing easy shots, half-assing sprints, icing fake injuries.

I'm almost not surprised when he doesn't show for Monday practice.

"That's weird," says Poltroni.

"Yeah," says Xavier.

Then Makarov misses two more. His locker is still there and his no-name sneakers are still there and his jocks are still there, but he isn't.

You seen Makarov?

Phones ring, doorbells buzz, no one knows shit. Suddenly there's MISSING! posters and HAVE YOU SEEN ME? leaflets and

REWARD! Xeroxes on every light pole in town. All week Coach Grout stands around gumming his whistle, until even he gets it.

Makarov isn't coming back.

Someone starts a rumor that Fitchburg had him kidnapped and that night their library is vandalized. Someone else claims they spotted Makarov at All-American Dog, and the next day forty people mill around the lot, eating footlongs and waiting for a sign. There's an article in the school paper that says Makarov had to go home to Republic of Whereverthefuck because of a coup. Or feudal uprising. Turns out he's from a royal family, enjoys a daily breakfast of borscht and bison vodka. The editor gets canned. The writer gets suspended. The MISSING! posters start to fade, replaced by arrogant cats and unlucky dogs.

It's all crap anyway.

The only truth is the West Boylston Bolts are nothing without him.

Hey Bolts! Go Screw!

We lose six in a row. Blown out by Temporal Catholic. Crushed by Rockwell Math and Science. Even lost a squeaker to Ulysses S. Grant, 114–66. The crowds disappear, the photogs disappear, all the feel-good disappears.

I call up Southern Community about my spot on the team, try to explain the collapse isn't my fault. Ring Ding says, "Don't worry, kid, you're still on my radar."

So we go back to squeezing our tools and joking around

under the bleachers during practice. Coach stops bothering to hide his flask. "Jump," he says a couple times, but no one listens. After a while he stops coming out of his office at all. Our last game of the season there's six people in the stands and five of them are Xavier's sisters. Coach has to prop himself against a scrub to keep from falling off the bench. We lose by 3 to Hammerchin Academy, the worst team in the state, a bunch of pasty jarheads grunting and shouting and trying really hard. I'm scoring from everywhere and have us in it right until the end. I spin and whirl, in a groove, hit from outside, take it to the rim, for the first time all year the best player on the floor.

It still isn't enough.

With ten seconds left I'm wide open in the corner. Washington makes a move, dribbles off his foot. The ball spins out of bounds. Game over. All the way to the locker room jarheads prong around us, laughing and hugging.

AFTER THE GAME, Steve's waiting outside, sunglasses on even though it's dark. The truck idles with attitude.

"How's it going?"

"It's going."

"You win?"

"No."

"How come?"

"Guess."

"You want a ride."

"With you?"

A WEEK LATER I get an envelope from Southern Community. Ring Ding can barely believe it himself, but two of his recruits blew out their knees and now he's got an open spot. Half scholarship plus board. It just needs a signature.

Am I still interested?

Underneath the paperwork is a stack of newspaper articles. They're from regional sports sections over the last decade, each one a variation on the same story. The first is about Aussie Jim Rhodes, surprise hoops phenom, who flew in from the deep Outback to single-handedly resurrect Small Time High. There's even a headshot of Aussie Jim, smiling.

Except it's Makarov.

The next is about Beau Candie, surprise hoops phenom, who flew in from Saskatchewan to single-handedly resurrect Somewhere Else High. There's a picture of Candie dunking.

Except it's Makarov.

There are more articles and more names. Francois LeMay. Knute Benzinger. Makarov without glasses, Makarov with unruly sideburns, Makarov with a gold grill and his name is Jody "Riff" Raft. Fucker is Peter Pan with hops and a great handle, has been shopping schools for years. Hey, why bother growing up when you can be a teenager forever, milk the glory, and then split as soon as anyone starts asking questions? A coach in Milwaukee is quoted as saying, "Hell, for all I know he's thirty-five and not even *from* Iceland. But man, the team sure does miss him."

Makarov created his own Comedy Hour. Except he was smart enough, even for a little while, to star in it.

At the bottom of the envelope is a Post-it note from Ring Ding with a chocolaty thumbprint in the corner: *I knew I recognized your man, so I did a little research. Wasn't so much his face as his jump shot. I never forget a jumper. Pathetic. Hope they catch him and string him up by the nuts. Anyway, like my stepdad always said: If it's too good to be true, it's too true to be good. We'll see you on campus, kid. And don't forget to bring some extra jocks. You can't have enough. My stepdad never said that, but if he had, he would have been right there too.*

THAT NIGHT I HEAR a mewling downstairs, like Dad forgot his sandwich again. But it's not Dad, it's Steve.

I open his door.

"You ever heard of knocking?"

His room hasn't changed since eighth grade. Zeppelin posters and titty girl cutouts and neon beer clocks. There are condom foils scattered under the bed like dried tulips. He's wearing boxers and a tight black shirt with the sleeves cut off, arms massive.

"Says the dude with a thousand secrets."

"I was going to tell you."

"Sure you were."

Steve nudges a stack of magazines with his toe. One of them slides to the floor, open to the centerfold, a gleaming yellow Chevy.

"So are you going to Southern Community or what?"

Honestly, I wasn't sure until right that second. And then the answer was so obvious it was like it'd been my plan all along.

"Nah, I'm done."

He looks up.

"With me?"

I want to say yes. Drop it like a depth charge, watch it explode against his starboard motor.

"No, man. With the team. Teams. Basketball. Fuck it."

Steve pulls a nubby blanket over his shoulders. I sit next to him on the bed. Out in the yard there's a rusty bicycle wheel, buried halfway up to the spokes.

"I guess you and I are supposed to have a talk now, right?" he says.

"Like some after-school special? All about accepting ourselves and shit?"

"Then you put your arm around me and everything's okay."

"Sure it is. A year later we open a business together."

"You get married, buy a house. I live in the barn out back."

"Right. Then there's a scene at Thanksgiving. I'm slicing the bird. You give me a look more meaningful than a dozen novels. My wife raises a glass of wine, says, *To family.* Roll credits."

He slides those perfect, dangling bangs behind one ear and I wonder how I could not have noticed, all this time.

That my brother has a tiny little scar on his chin.

"Seriously though, dude?"

"What?"

"Did Makarov ever tell you his real name?"

Steve wipes his nose on my shirt, face puffy and oblivious.

"What do you mean?"

Snap!

"Nevermind," I say, and go get us two of Dad's beers.

So WASHINGTON GETS accepted to Purdue and sells me his car for twelve hundred and an ounce of pot. Poltroni gets married and moves to the city to manage his dad's meat warehouse. Xavier joins the air force and gets stationed in the North Pole or somewhere.

For a while I keep it up with the doggie bags and the bus pans, then after Christmas put in for sous chef. Georgie clears it with Diamond Spatula and eventually takes me on as an apprentice. He says I've got perfect hands, big and soft. Also, I work at night, which means I never miss Comedy Hour. Matter of fact, I'm parked there right now. You should hear the rumble of the .351, idling behind the Dumpster. You should see the parade of students, fresh and scrubbed and oblivious as ever, each centered in a gleaming silver frame. You should see the kid who wears an eye patch as he comes pounding through the tunnel, the way he grips the wheel, hunched over, a look on his face that knows even when he's fifty the pirate jokes will never end.

Snap!

"It's beautiful," Steve says.

It's true. It really is.

I light two cigarettes and we exhale at the same time, twin plumes that fill the car with smoke.

Base Omega
Has Twelve Dictates

We get nailed. Right outside the fence. Mainly because Young Nick Drake's trench coat snags on the razor wire and he refuses to split without it, dangling like that Christmas ornament you leave in the box every year but never throw away.

I'm like, "Dude, time? In terms of it running out?"

And he's like, "Just go without me."

So I yank his ankles until the seam rips, which wakes Jeff and Pink Lady, who set off the mayo jar alarms and pretty soon all of Base Omega surrounds us with pointy sticks and accusatory eyes. Are we by any chance heading for the long-rumored New Lagos? Have we buried a secret hoard over the next dune filled with cocktail wieners and cans of savory V8?

"No way," I say.

"Of course not," Young Nick Drake says.

BULLSHIT, Dorsal Vent writes in the sand.

Mom sends Bob Her New Boyfriend Who Swears He Didn't Kill Dad to go and wake Larry Our Leader, who comes out of his yurt wearing nothing but muscles and biker boots, looking very sleepy.

As well as grievously betrayed.

"Set up the wheel," he says. "It's spinning time."

WE HAD A DOG N THOUGHT IT WOULD PROTECT US. WE HAD A GUN N THOUGHT IT WOULD PROTECT US. WE HAD A DAD AND (AT LEAST I) THOUGHT HE WAS GONNA PROTECT US.
—graffiti at base of Mandalay Bay fountain

STOP PRETENDING THIS IS A MOVIE AND YOU'RE TOUGH. YOU'RE NOT TOUGH AND THIS ISN'T A MOVIE.
—graffiti at base of MGM Grand pyramid

KRUA, I CAN'T LIVE WITHOUT YOU. LET'S JUMP THE FENCE AND ESCAPE TOGETHER.
—graffiti on a rock just outside the fence

My name's Krua, which is exactly the sort of dumbass handle your mom saddles you with postcollapse, hoping one day you become a "strong warrior woman" + rule the wasteland or whatever. I am not a woman. I'm twelve. Who rules the sun? Who rules the sand? I'm also not psychic or insanely smart or descended from an ancient royal bloodline. I'm just this way-too-tan girl robbed of shopping for her first bra by the apocalypse. So, no, I will not discover a lost city or learn to commune with friendly buzzards or battle other twelve-year-olds in a special televised battle arena to save my little sister or tribe. If only because, hey, little sister died of infected tooth/bored resignation months ago and our "tribe" is forty (possibly thirty-nine by the end of this sentence) exhausted people in Base Omega.

Which is really just a parking lot with a fence.

It's like *The Last of the Dehydrated Peas, Since There Sure Ain't No Mohicans Left.*

Base Omega features lots of arguments about tarps. Plus sunburn, expiring of ignoble diarrhea, and only minor cannibalism. Also, a big surge in rapish assault, always from behind (bad breath) followed by nervous pacing and a canine's shifty regret. Sometimes an apology, sometimes not. Sometimes a revenge puncturing, sometimes not. Lucky Omegans live in old cars. Unlucky ones live in the shade of old cars. Almost no one wears fingerless leather gloves or empty bandoliers anymore. They barely remember why they're so tired (ambient radiation) or why their family is gone (not enough rat sushi/only one chopstick) or why they can't seem to rub two thoughts together (crankcase water=high benzene content).

Either way, Mom and Bob Her New Boyfriend Who Swears He Didn't Kill Dad say we're lucky to have found such a terrific home.

Lucky is relative. Most relatives are dead.

And no, I'm not hot. Random pervs and furtive yankers can stop reading right here because at no point will I take off my glasses, slip into a perfectly preserved wedding dress, and become Jennifer Lawrence.

Dudes, I haven't brushed my teeth in *years*.

IN FEBRUARY I was promoted to Keeper of the Dictates. The dictates are written on skin that could conceivably be pig. In case you didn't know, dictates are inviolable rules. In case you didn't know, inviolable means sacrosanct. In case you didn't know, sacrosanct comes from the Latin *sac*, which there's a real shortage of dangling between Omega legs.

We have Tribal Caucus every Friday in the Grieving Yurt. It's totally boring, except when I'm called on to recite dictates in support of motions. Motions are sometimes about More Food or Don't Just Leave Poop or Who Remembers Knitting? But most often they're about how Larry Wants That Thing You've Just Hidden. Like an earring. Or glasses with a single lens. Or a TAG Heuer inscribed "To my little hole-in-one" permanently frozen at 5:16. Complainers tend to get a spin of the wheel, so usually they just hand over the swag. Besides, Larry's greed is vital. Without someone to unreasoningly hate and foment never-executed plots against, would Base Omega even bother to man the lookout posts anymore? Would we deign to boil sop water, bait lizard snares, or spend predawn hours searching the burning desert for the last few scraps left to burn?

Yeah, probably not.

THE TWELVE DICTATES

(As told to Larry by God. Or in this case,
to Larry by Larry after huffing too much Freon.)

1. No worshiping graven images. No worship at all.

At first there was the whole bible thing, your various Korans and Upanishads. Liturgy. Verses. Knees on rocks beseeching, hands raised toward the sky. But results were minimal, so they got chucked. The subsequent Mother Earth/Gaia routine was a total nonstarter. Old gods and oracles were a big *meh*. Then things devolved a bit. Sacrifices. Robes and chants. Entrails and augurs and meaning to be found in random spatters of blood. "Not much meaning, too much mess" was the feeling in the end. Turns out there's just no way to roast the family Doberman with a delicate sand marinade and still embrace the almighty. Small questions need small answers. The big lesson of apocalypse is that what we really used to worship was the idea that no matter how bad things got, some uniform would eventually drive up in a jeep and save us.

Politicians? Marines? The crucified son?

No one's coming.

2. All decisions will be made by Larry. Got a beef, chief? You're welcome to caucus a more equitable third-party solution on the other side of the fence.

Young Nick Drake says this is a foolish policy. He says partisan dickering is what started deep dystopia to begin with. Also, Ayn Rand. He says there are no solutions, but there is a better life out there.

I don't believe him.

"I don't believe you."

"It's true," he says, his sad, gentle eyes sadder and gentler than usual.

Jeff and Pink Lady, who sit in a '71 Torino all day, say I'm being a fool. Jeff makes theoretical origami swans while Pink Lady rakes his chest hair with a fork. They think Young Nick Drake is full of it. "We don't need no consensus, we just need someone to be right for once," they say. I'd like to study the question, but the selection in the Camry Lending Library is limited. And heavy on Augusten Burroughs. Even so, I'm pretty sure there was zero time for an airing of diverse perspectives the night a horde of kidney-gnawers stormed the fence with ear necklaces and femur torches.

Young Nick Drake thought we should let them in, negotiate.

Jeff and Pink Lady locked themselves in the Torino's trunk.

Larry yelled, "Poke 'em through the links with sharp sticks!"

Which worked.

After that he was in charge.

3. To avoid abuses of power that will prove irresistible to even the most wizened leader, said leader can be overruled at any

*time by the checking balance of the Cabinet of Women. Base
Omega formally recognizes that bigoted, entitled white men are
responsible for the entirety of our plight and have always been
the resource-sucking plunderers that certain websites once had
the fortitude to point out. The early pagans were correct: ma-
triarchy is the natural order of things. Chicks is smarter than
dicks.*

However, granting women a voice in decision making and
then institutionally ignoring them is actually sort of comforting, a familiar precollapse blanket. After being elected leader
of the Cabinet of Women, Dorsal Vent wrote, "Being teased
by inclusiveness and then cruelly shut out reminds me of
Christmas morning." Dorsal Vent is a former escort with a
weird cut on her neck that at first everyone took for a gill-slit,
a harbinger of our collective impending mutation. Even Larry
Our Leader was sure we'd soon morph into semiamphibious
quadrupeds, and so a mildly hysterical Base Omega spent
weeks obsessing over various moles and armpit lumps.

"How can we be amphibious in the desert?" Jeff asked.

"Will my gill-slit breathe sand?" Pink Lady asked.

"This is just the sort of hysteria that keeps us from ac-
complishing the simplest of goals or improving our situation
in any way," Young Nick Drake said. "Which, unfortunately,
points to a vacuum in leadership."

"Quiet," I whispered, but Young Nick Drake just spoke
louder.

"My friends, if we cannot express ourselves plainly here, in the apocalypse, then why bother having mouths at all?"

Larry fumed, twirled his scepter, marched around with that Someone Wants a Taste of the Wheel look until I ran for the Freon rag and lured him back to his yurt.

But Young Nick Drake was right about one thing: turns out Dorsal Vent's vent was just old pimp retribution un-inclined to heal, which she insisted all along, but no one listened.

Because, really, what else would a mutant say?

4. Fuck your own gender, Base Omega. Gay is okay! In fact, it's a massive biological advantage. Just keep your dance moves to yourself, Alphonso. Just don't put any cilantro on Larry's rat-on-a-stick, Julian.

At first, Base Omega was all, *Hey folks, forget outdated societal norms concerning public fornication and scripture-based monogamy, we need to repopulate, stat!* Larry's favorite affirmation was *Don't waste it in the sand, go ahead and put that seed in a pal!* But then one morning we woke up and three women were pregnant (four if you count Pink Lady, who kept shoving a pillow under her dress) and suddenly Base Omega was all, *Oh, shit, we need a doctor! Plus vitamins and less-restrictive maternity wardrobes!* Base Omega was all, *Exactly who in this godforsaken sand pile is going to provide basic health services, let alone comprehensive postnatal care?*

Six months later the preemies all came together, as if by pre-arranged signal, pushed between bloody thighs and into the dirt. Base Omega was all, *No, you bite the umbilical cord!* Even so, the babies were hearty and thrived. Tiny miracles! At least until Osiris disappeared without a peep, his bucket-seat crib empty and undisturbed. Base Omega was stumped. Maybe God lifted him back to heaven on a silken throw pillow? But then Ranxerox was dragged off by a reptile that Jeff and Pink Lady swore was the size of a German shepherd. During the Day of Uncontrollable Crying, while a twenty-four-hour detail was formed to watch over Aegisth, she seems to have spontaneously combusted. All that was left was a tiny briquette, still warm, like it was just waiting for a match and stalk of mesquite.

After that, Base Omega was all, *Fuck this shit*, and, *Hey, no one get pregnant again, ever. Okay? Please?*

The future is frottage.

5. There will be games.

Every Sunday during Low Radiation Season there's a tournament + festivities. Four teams, one bracket. The lizard jerky stores are plundered, and someone unearths two fingers of backwashed Johnnie Walker. Jeff wears his lucky cummerbund. Pink Lady puts on her was-once-paisley frock. The Penalty Box is filled with soup cans and rusty scissors.

Young Nick Drake refuses to join in.

Young Nick Drake says sports are an anachronistic vestige of the blood plunder of black lives, a sweatshop of concussions and splintered bone, and that the continued thirst for random violence after the Collapse is something any decent apocalypse would repudiate.

Larry laughs and says Young Nick Drake is just mad because he was picked last.

Larry laughs and says Young Nick Drake throws like a girl.

Young Nick Drake begs me not to play.

"Why?"

"I'm scared you'll get hurt."

A tear rolls down his cheek.

An actual tear. In the middle of the desert. He dabs it and rests it on the tip of my tongue as the Clanging Pot of Beginning clangs.

I make it to the opening ceremonies just in time. There are fireworks (throwing lots of sand in the air) and a speech from Larry Our Leader about not hiding random scavenge from Larry Our Leader (*You tell them LOL!*).

Then Dorsal Vent rolls out the first iguana bladder.

I play for Team So What. We're young and fast. Bob Her New Boyfriend Who Swears He Didn't Kill Dad plays for Team Dreaming of Waffles. They're old and slow. It's the first to a dozen, win by two. Winners get double rations for a week. Losers are sent on Go Hike Twenty Miles Looking for Food That Isn't There patrol.

Last year's losers never came back.

Same with the year before.

The smart money is not on Team Dreaming of Waffles.

6. Do you really give a crap about #6? No, you want to hear more about Young Nick Drake.

Fine. He's fifteen. He has soulful green eyes and a wispy goatee and plays delicate songs about collapse and redemption on the lizard-tendon guitar. He wears a black trench coat, always, even in the worst of the heat. Jeff and Pink Lady say it's because he's hiding a gill slit. So not! Young Nick Drake speaks with a delicate lisp and lives in a '68 Citroën that smells like old man hospital sac (which he burns various desert herbs to get rid of, but only makes it smell 40 percent more like old man hospital sac + lightly seared with new potatoes and pistachio chutney). Young Nick Drake sits near the Dictate Crate during tribal meetings and stares at me with an expression that says he'd happily carry all of apocalypse on his thin shoulders if I'd only ask.

Which makes it hard to concentrate.

Jeff and Pink Lady say, "We don't trust him! He's not one of us! You know nothing about his sensitive poet ass!"

Which is true, because Young Nick Drake refuses to say anything at all about his past except that his sister jumped off the Ninety-Seventh floor of an unnamed Steve Wynn property two days after the Collapse. And I only know that because it's also the chorus of his best song, "My Sister Jumped

Off the Ninety-Seventh Floor of an Unnamed Steve Wynn Property Two Days After the Collapse Blues."

Base Omega was all, *Yeah, chief, that's a real sad story.*

Base Omega was all, *Yeah, champ, that's totally tragic.*

But they knocked off the crap once Young Nick Drake strummed those gila tendons around the campfire. Then Base Omega nodded in time and sang along with the catchy hooks and hooky melodies and forgot that they didn't trust Young Nick Drake as far as they could throw him, which probably wasn't high enough to clear the fence anyway.

Young Nick Drake tells me he's working on a brand new song.

A ballad.

He says it's called "Krua by the Glow of a Thousand Burning Well Fires."

Sure, it's pure corn.

But there are times when I watch his fingers *ping ping ping* over the strings, nails polished black with melted tar, lips parted wetly in song, and think, well, you know, *maybe.*

7. Stealing is venal. Thieves will be flayed. Food thieves will spend a week in the Box. Minus a hand.

The Box is really just the trunk of a Kia Sorento buried up to the wheel wells next to Base Omega's latrine. Which is really just the camper shell of an Isuzu Trooper dragged over a hole in the tar that's not nearly deep enough.

It gets *hot* in the box.

It *smells* in the latrine.

No one really steals anymore.

Especially left-handed.

8. Base Omega will each memorize a work of classic literature to ensure that we do not lose touch with our vital literary traditions and a connection to the higher arts.

Larry Our Leader got the idea from a graphic novel called *Fahrenheit 451*. Lizard bones were drawn from a beret. Jeff and Pink Lady pulled John Cheever. Dorsal Vent got Gertrude Stein. Crazy Apron Alice made a run at *Green Eggs and Ham*. But after a few days of laborious mumbling, Base Omega was all, *Wait, what was the problem with burning books again?*

Young Nick Drake got *Naked Lunch* and immediately had the exterminator parts down pat, could quote Dr. Benway in a Dr. Benway voice that even Larry Our Leader said was creepier than a run of bad Freon.

I memorized the first four pages of *Madame Bovary* and walked around for a month like, *Monsieur Roger, I have brought you a new boy*, and, *You may now discard your helmet, young fop*, but it turns out even the future hates Flaubert. Base Omega was all, *We're fine to lose touch with that French pussy*. Base Omega was all, *Fuck books, their pathetic reliance on recycled plots and ill-considered foreshadowing are no longer germane to our rapidly changing world. Besides, we're tired and bored and would give almost anything for a chipotle-braised organic pork medallion right now.*

I'm like, *Wait, what* wouldn't *you give?*

Base Omega was all, *We would happily rekill our dead mothers for a chipotle-braised organic pork medallion right now.*

9. *All Base Omegans will be trained in self-defense and the use of modern weaponry.*

At first it was guns, guns, guns. But that didn't last. Ever try to fire a TEC-9 full of sand? Ever watch a movie where the hero's pistol never runs out of hollow points? Here's how the real apocalypse works: for the first seventy-two hours everyone left is terrified to the point of raggedy psychosis, so they shoot at whatever blinks, farts, or moves, and by Wednesday are out of ammo.

Even people smart enough to stockpile have to waste their stockpiles killing people dumb enough to try and take their stockpiles away.

Guns = hunks of metal not good for much except tenderizing rat meat.

It turns out the best possible weapon in the future is a sharpened length of galvanized pipe. Preferably about five feet long. The key to dystopic combat is not Korean assault rifles or suppressing fire or slow-motion kicks, it's a Medium-Deep Puncture.

In the end, we are the thinnest of balloons filled with organy pudding, just waiting to be popped. Get stuck with a sharpened length of galvanized pipe and you might not die right away, but you will soon after. Sepsis sets in almost immediately. There's no surgery, no fighting off infection, no antibiotics, no wrapping strips of dirty sheet around the wound and somehow it's fine the next day. It's infected the next day. It's gangrene the day after that.

Get poked = you die.

So Pink Lady teaches Weapons N' Tactics. Dorsal Vent leads Take Back the Night self-defense class.

Of course, Young Nick Drake refuses to train at all.

"I am committed to nonviolence."

It makes Larry Our Leader very mad.

"If it helps, I'm happy to lead a Conflict Resolution seminar instead."

Larry Our Leader is fairly certain that conflict cannot ever be resolved.

"Well, let's just see who shows up."

I am the only one who shows up.

Young Nick Drake puts away his notes, refolds the folding chair, and then leads me by the hand across the compound.

"Where are we going?"

"The Camry Lending Library."

In the backseat Young Nick Drake leans very close, reaches into his pocket.

And presents me with a gift.

It's so beautiful.

So perfect.

A rolled up tube of Crest X-Tra White that's got, easily, two squeezes left.

It goes a very long way toward resolving our biggest conflict.

10. *Never make out with Young Nick Drake.*

His chin whiskers tickle. He strokes my neck softly and whispers my name with a longing that transcends the end of the world and everything in it.

"Krua. Oh, Krua."

"If we're going to be friends," I say, trembling, "you're gonna have to knock it off with that shit. My real name's Sandy."

Young Nick Drake kisses my knuckles. He kisses my filthy little fingertips. He wraps the empty toothpaste tube around my third finger like a ring.

"Does this mean we're engaged?"

He winks and says, "Sandy, we gotta get out of this place."

He says, "I know somewhere we can be alone, pitch our own decoratively embroidered yurt."

He says, "I'll be Romeo and you be Milla Jovovich."

"But what's wrong with Base Omega?" I whisper.

He shakes his head as if I'm a child.

"Isn't it obvious? Larry's insane."

I wonder if it is obvious. Or maybe just predictable.

"We have to go, Krua," he hisses. "Like, tonight."

11. All empires invariably collapse, from Byzantium to Egypt to Vegas. And usually with a whimper of irrelevance. Except this one.

Larry Our Leader calls me to his yurt, asks what I think Dictate Eleven means. I tell him I couldn't even hazard a guess.

He waits, slapping at insects that aren't there.

So I say if forced to hazard at stick-point, Dictate Eleven suggests we're nothing but vague organic amalgams, random cells made flesh, whose interior mechanics have no real purpose except to slowly degrade until they fail.

He takes a mighty huff of Freon, grins redly.

"Excellent. Continue."

I tell him that the reign of any society is merely the interstices prior to its collapse. That all thought systems fall apart, philosophical conceptions nothing but buzzard carcasses waiting to rot and be replaced. I say that even Apocalypse Now eventually becomes Apocalypse Then.

In other words, we're all just a big pile of crap.

"Sure. But why sentient crap?"

It's a good point.

Larry gets up from the rusty architect's table where he spends all day drawing pictures of displeased Asian women. He's nude, oiled from head to toe.

"You're a good girl, Krua. A real asset to Base Omega."

It is clear that Larry does not believe this.

"One day you will lead us."

It is clear that I will never lead us.

"But you seem distracted. Like there's something you want to tell me."

On the oak dresser is Larry's collection of used candy wrappers. I hold a scrunch of plastic to my nose, inhale the scent of vintage Twix.

"I'm going to find out either way."

We're practically touching. My forehead comes up to his neck. Heat radiates from his sunburn. A lust for something far more complicated than lust exudes from every pore.

I try to keep my mouth shut, but it's hard. Larry's eyes beam directly into my skull, searching for lies. I have to give him something real, something true.

"Before the Collapse my father used to wake me every morning by making fart noises on my belly button with his lips. Then he'd say, 'You must rise, my little pumpkin, but I give you permission not to shine.'"

Larry shakes his head, disappointed.

"The boy, Krua. His plan."

A rusty knife is sunk to the shaft in the Eames bed stand. Several lengths of sharpened galvanized pipe lean against the wet bar.

I know Larry knows I'm considering them.

He grips my shoulder, squeezes way too hard.

"You're a very lucky girl, Krua. Do you know why?"

"No."

"Because I am giving you a gift much more valuable than

toothpaste. I'm allowing you to make a choice. Do you remember the baboons?"

I did. A year ago a pack of them appeared on the fence. Perched along the razor wire. They croaked and spit and scratched. At first Base Omega was excited, thinking we could trap and eat them. But then the baboons started throwing excrement. Which was watery and neon red. Also, they all had both sex parts. And weren't shy with the flashing and fiddling. Larry said it meant they were a bad omen, pumped full of toxic effluent. He said Base Omega might as well cram down a plate of Fukushima fajitas. Twee Rob, a former kindergarten adjunct with a passion for artisanal cheese and locally sourced vests, disagreed. He twirled his mustache and said, "Au contraire, mi amigo!" He said he could prepare the beasts correct, just like how sushi chefs serve blowfish, which are poison if you don't know exactly where to slice, but are otherwise this prized delicacy. Twee Rob managed to impale one of the healthier-looking baboons with a sharpened galvanized pole and then slow-roasted it for many hours.

"See!" he said, crunching through the first chunk, as wonderful-smelling juices ran out the corners of his mouth and dangled from his beard.

Everyone laughed, wanting some too, and began to fight over Omega Plate and Omega Spoon.

Until Twee Rob screamed. Until foam bubbled from between his teeth. Until his eyes flipped inside-out.

And then he exploded.

So, maybe Larry Our Leader knows what he's talking about. Maybe he's the person who's right for once.

"I choose you," I whisper.

His grin is a dissertation on the Tartar of the Future.

"Good. In the end we must all follow our heart. For it is a very lonely hunter."

"Flannery O'Connor?"

"No, Carson McCullers. But I always get them mixed up, too."

He takes another huff of Freon.

"Now get the fuck out of my yurt."

12. *No one leaves Base Omega. Ever.*

I knock softly on the Citroën's window, but Young Nick Drake is already awake.

"I knew you'd come."

His guitar is slung over his shoulder, some trinkets tied into a square of rag.

"Now what?" I whisper.

"Now we carpe the diem, baby."

We cross the compound in a running crouch, from Audi to Peugeot to Pinto. We loop behind the latrine to avoid Pink Lady, who's on watch, and to avoid Jeff, who watches Pink Lady. The moon is up and full. Its light feels irradiated. There are few places to hide, long shadows cast in every direction. But we're lucky and make it to the spot where the kidney-gnawers once attacked, where the razor wire is bent and slightly lowered.

I throw a blanket across the spiky rampart, grab two links and flip myself over, land cleanly on the other side.

Young Nick Drake winks, goes next.

WE'RE FORCED TO KNEEL, arms tied firmly behind our backs.

Larry Our Leader yawns.

"Spin that shit."

"Spin the wheel! Spin the wheel!" Base Omega chants, as the wheel is dragged to the middle of the compound. Torches are lit. Everyone gathers around the colored triangles and rickety axle and clackity stopper, which apparently once topped a tricky par 3 at North Vegas Mini-Golf.

Dorsal Vent gets a good grip on the pegs and sends the disc whirring.

Clackity clackity clack clack . . . clack . . . clack . . . clack.

The pointer almost lands on CRUCIFUCKTION.

Just barely makes it past WELCOME TO THE JUNGLE.

Neither are good options.

But both are better than GRIEVOUSLY BETRAYED REDRESS STEW, where it finally stops.

There's twenty seconds of horrified silence.

And then Base Omega begins to chant.

"Grievously Betrayed Redress Stew! Grievously Betrayed Redress Stew!"

"And so it shall be," Larry Our Leader says.

The Sanctifying Salt and Pepper are quickly found. A fire is lit. For the next simmery twelve hours, Base Omegans who are otherwise squeamish close their eyes and hum ditties, tell themselves that if you looked at it less factually and more like cartoons hallucinated during an unmedicated fugue state, Young Nick Drake could really be a lean little billy goat found frolicking in the desert.

Which is probably to some degree accurate.

In the end, I didn't get to have any stew.

Mainly since I spent the next seven days in the Box.

I don't think I could've eaten anyway.

All week, late at night, as I lay there with arms and legs numb and tongue swollen and flecked white, Larry leaned against the Kia trunk and whispered.

"As we evolve beyond the sort of people who once fetishized cell phones and spent their lives revenging playground slights by acquiring powerfully red cars, we have to decide who we are going to be now. Right this moment. Here in the irradiated zone. Behavior does not change. People do not change. History does not change. Only the weather changes. Are you prepared to be the weather, Krua?"

"It's like, I am literally about to die of thirst here."

LOL chuckles. "Yes, but assuming you don't, you tiny chunk of meat, what are you going to be from this point forward? A filet that I can trust? Or one that I need to debone with malice?"

"So totally trust. I swear."

When they finally let me out, I drink a '77 Impala's worth

of crankcase water and sleep for a week. Then, when I can walk again, I have to learn how to do everything all over. Left-handed. Like write and wipe my asshole.

Also, now I'm comic relief at Tribal Caucus, because I keep dropping the parchment.

Larry Our Leader laughs and says, "You're my left-hand man."

The rest of Base Omega laughs with him.

I go to give them the finger, realize I'm giving them the stump.

GOOD ONE, Dorsal Vent writes in the sand.

And then we do roll-call, announce our names and purposes.

When it's my turn I stand in front of all of Base Omega and say, in a clear voice that rings out across the desert morning, "I am Krua, Keeper of the Dictates."

Exposure

6:12 A.M.

The peeling Victorian sits north of Cesar Chavez and south of a Safeway lot, on a street called Guerrero, which means "war," three lanes of nonstop traffic and no good bars to speak of. Two flats, two stories. Connected by a wobbly staircase, by the ever-present smell of wet rug and spilled soy and unstable neighbor. There's a crayoned wall and a stack of detective magazines and a fireplace piled high with dead flowers. There's a dozen roommates who call each other flatmates, an apartment they call a commune. I hear them all from my center room, the laughter, anger, orgasm. I feel them from my spot on the floor, vibrations rising through the joists, random lives under cheap planks and the rusty nails that run the length of my spine.

8:40 A.M.

Johnny, who lives across the hall.

"Good morning."

"Hi."

Johnny, with his beard and slippers and trucker's belly, looking down at me, worried.

"Why are you lying on the floor?"

"No reason."

"Aren't you cold without any clothes?"

"A little."

Johnny, depressed, on my couch with a crumpled tissue, telling stories, boyfriends come and go, have come and gone.

"You'll be all right," I say.

He nods, flips through my record collection, the last eight or ten left, a Human League and a Ramones, some other stuff.

"You mind if I play "Fever" again?"

"Not at all."

He lifts the needle.

Johnny, who loves Peggy Lee.

9:12 A.M.

Susan, who collects the rent and arranges house meetings. Who drapes a towel over my hips before she can speak.

"Need some help getting up?"

The floor is splintered in circles, lacquer worn away. Someone plays the old piano, a barely realized minuet.

"No, thanks."

"Listen," she says, trying to smile and falling short. "I

don't want to pry, but is this something that could involve the cops?"

Susan, with the three best rooms, a hoarder. Floor to ceiling boxes, beads, bolts of fabric, doll heads, gears and wires, newspapers stacked and snipped, paper-clipped articles about Squeaky Fromme and Victor Mature and Shirley Chisholm.

"I doubt it."

She looks out the window. There's broken machinery in the garden, compost unattended, a small patch of cement yard, more cigarette butt than cement. The fog settles around a city that believes its own clichés, practically crop-dusted gray.

"Listen, I don't want to pry, but if you're just going to lie there, how are you going to pay rent?"

11:22 A.M.

Irene, who wears a fedora and studies Foucault. Irene, with random scraggly hairs that will never flourish into a beard. Irene in a Che shirt, toasting her birthday with a hammer-and-sickle cupcake that arrived packed in dry ice. Irene who steals kerosene for the generator, siphons it from a barrel behind the French restaurant with a length of rubber hose. Irene who burned a VR FOR VICTORY insignia into the front lawn, said it stood for Volta Redonda, the Amazonian hamlet she intended to machete her way down to by Christmas in order to found a Utopian colony based on the precepts of Eldridge Cleaver.

"Direct action is the only sane response," she says, and then gives the Black Power salute.

Noon

Terry and Trish who thumbed from North Carolina, the sounds of rutting from the room above. Terry with his three-string guitar, two-string drawl, black turtleneck. You can take the seed out of the hay but not the hay out of the seed.

"Don't you wanna eat a hamburger? Don't you wanna get up and see a matinee? Damn, boy, are you even *alive*?"

Terry, sweating and chewing his crank-lip, clomping around me in circles, the white-boy duckwalk, pretending to play Chuck Berry on a broom.

Trish, long and straight and auburn, who carries scissors in her purse "just in case," a smile that says she can't wait. Trish, standing in my doorway in a T-shirt and panties. "I could get you a blanket."

"No, thanks."

"I could rub your shoulders."

"No, thanks."

Trish, throwing things at Terry's head, a good aim, his dented skull.

"That woman thinks she's Orel Hershizzer."

Trish with a laugh like a tubercular mule.

"That is *so* funny, HEE *HAR*."

Terry, who had to be bailed out, blood on the door.

2:36 P.M.

Bryan, the rumor, the roomer. Bryan with extensions piled like an understudy for *Carmen*. Bryan in bare feet and loose pants, taut, halfway between dangerous and not.

"Monday's my recital."

"Wonderful."

Bryan sweeping into my room to stretch, one leg extended, mastering the Alexander technique in a crouch against the wall. He contorts, twists, a spasm of muscle, suddenly over me.

"For real, though. What are you doing?"

"Nothing."

"Is it, like, some kind of boycott?"

I don't answer, watch him pirouette, lower into an impossible split.

"I guess this means you can't make my recital?"

"I'd like to. But probably no."

Bryan, twirling away to his room full of plants, his radio, banjos or drums or ululating Arabs. Bryan disappearing for a week then coming back reincarnated, insisting his new name is Ariel.

3:09 P.M.

Highguy, who wants to start a techno band with two laptops and four grams of coke. It'll be called Storming Kabul. He'll be Ace Storming and I'll be Billy Kabul. He'll be vocals and I'll be drums. He'll be right back and I'll be waiting.

4:17 P.M.

Sasha, elaborately dreadlocked, bored, in bangles and cheap jewelry, the real stones in some Manhattan safe box that will open on her thirtieth birthday. Sasha, who squats at my side, shows yards of white thigh, wants to *really talk*, wash her feet in the Euphrates.

"You ever wonder if there's a purpose?"

"Yes."

"You ever wonder what happens after?"

"Certainly."

"You ever wonder why we're even here?"

"Many times."

"I don't mean in this house."

"I know what you mean."

She arranges her skirts, runs her finger around me like a chalk outline.

"Is it yoga? Meditation?"

"Om," I say.

She laughs, then stops, worried it was the wrong thing. Her shirt falls away, shoulder draped with a ruinous tattoo, an enormous lizard playing the stand-up bass, the idea of some drummer who dumped her over the phone.

5:05 P.M.

Tom, who's on a tight allowance after Susan cashes his SSI. Tom, who smokes like it's his only tether, who runs out of Bugler midmonth and then will roll anything, lint, leaves, dust, hair. Tom, who talks to the sconces, berates the wainscoting, describes the damask. Tom, who giggles into his jacket sleeve, an ancient blue pinstripe, who paints canvases of stacked eyeballs in intestinal caverns, more Gacy than Van

Gogh, more Manson than Warhol. Tom, who got lost in the park and lived for a week off a jar of salsa. Tom, who knows he's not allowed in my room but likes to peek in anyway.

6:54 P.M.

Red and Miriam, married. Miriam over forty and Red maybe twenty-five. Red, with an ancient Volvo and greasy hand-shake. Red who took me to an apple festival where we polished off a sack of Royal Galas and watched clog dancers spin in bonnets.

Miriam embarrassed. "Red's got an old soul."

"You don't need to explain."

"I'm not trying to."

Miriam, round and vaguely menacing, who claims to be a nurse, who has a room full of tinctures and concoctions, a gynecological exam table from the twenties. Straps and wires. Studded leg stirrups.

"It's an antique."

Miriam, prepared to inject remedies, insert vitamins. Spansules and suppositories. Aminos and lysines and B12.

"I can start you on a course of antibiotics right now."

"I'll pass."

She shakes her head, repacks her tools. "Suit yourself."

"I won't come crying," I say, half a beat before she says, "Don't come crying."

The stairs creak, with her weight and all its intent.

9:01 P.M.

Gareth, pale and ropey-huge, shaved head and thick Buddy Holly glasses, like a Marine in Da Nang in 1962. Gareth, whose own little slice of anarchy is refusing to scrub the pans and then taking his shirt off if it's such a problem. Gareth, whose favorite tangent is on the evils of sampling, but also how Minor Threat was so overrated. Gareth, who has read *Zen and the Art of Motorcycle Maintenance* three times and can quote thoughtful passages. Who is positive global warming is a hippie conspiracy and that London skins have a secret and one day he'll fly to Kings Row and learn what it is.

Gareth, whose obliviousness is like cologne, a pent boy in a soldier's body, a walking slogan misheard or dimly understood, curiosity masturbated into submission.

Gareth, wound so tight he's practically backwards.

Gareth who stares, shakes his head, slams the door. Twice.

MIDNIGHT

Cassandra, mixed-race, whip-tight, a bike messenger in riding shorts. Cassandra smelling like a dray horse, rubbing my forehead.

"My mother has a new husband. This one's white, too."

"Rich?"

"She lays around all day in a satin robe."

"Like Eartha Kitt?"

"No, like you."

Cassandra, who takes me in her arms sometimes, dark

nest scratching my back. We spoon, chaste, warm one another. But not tonight.

"Sorry, but I'm not getting down on the floor."

"I don't blame you."

Cassandra, who wears tube socks like debutante gloves. Who has a horizontal scar under one eye that only makes her more beautiful.

3:56 A.M.

My wife, who figured if we went and talked to a woman with a suspect degree and scented candles and paid two hundred an hour, it would get better. If we sold her mother's house and took a cruise up the Adriatic and toasted with glasses of Retsina on various balconies, it would all become clear. Who thought there were zones of unexplored erogeny whose erogeny wasn't forever dissipated by calling them "zones." Who thought a triple-A Duracell would power a reawakening between us somewhere along the magnitude of Loma Prieta and the rise of Cthulhu.

My wife, who eventually gave up and said, "Fine, leave," put me on the Greyhound with a packed lunch.

The diesel groaned away from Florida, packed, a welter of sweat and raw dumbness, a box full of tight hats. Six days of sandwiches and bourbon, a thousand miles of gravel. Texas then Chicago, highway pickets and billboards and dirty snow, Boulder then Salt Lake, sixty seats and sixty feet and two bumpers. The port of Oakland as it rose behind steel containers labeled in Chinese, and then cold Market Street, which lay unloved between the spread legs of downtown San Francisco.

Schoolgirls slapped each other's lollipops to the sidewalk, *Hey, bitch, hey!*

Traffic accelerated through the yield.

The sidewalk was oddly impacted with gum, a black-pock Braille. There were posters with warnings about a new flesh-eating disease, a guy bumming change with a canoe missing from his thigh, a big chunk gone pink, marbled deep to bone.

I had two drinks in a bar where some men were painting an Aztec warrior on the wall, slept in an all-night laundry for a week, across ridged orange seats bolted to the floor.

"Hey, buddy, you can't lie there."

"My sweater is on spin."

"Beat it."

I took pictures at random, shutter exposing actual film, a place downtown you could rent darkrooms by the hour, the guy at the desk offering two hundred for my grandfather's Leica.

A Rasta with paperbacks laid out on a blanket said, "You need a place to live?" and when I said, "Yeah," closed his eyes and said, "Try the grocery that sell the green drinks."

Next to the juicer was an index card taped to the wall, CHEAP ROOM.

It said, *HI! DO YOU PREFER TO LIVE AS A COMMUNITY?*

No.

SHARE MEALS AND CHORES AND EXPERIENCES?

Not really.

ARE YOU LOOKING FOR SOMETHING DIFFERENT?

Than what?

$260 A MONTH. COOK ONCE A WEEK. NOT SCARED OF VEGAN, WICCAN, OR AIDS.

I moved in the next day, found a job as an attendant to a man who was very rich, who had one of those illnesses where you're perfectly healthy.

I wheeled him to clothing stores and movies, made him grilled cheese and sliced oranges, indexed his receipts and wiped his chin.

I met my roommates, went to baseball games alone, froze, spilled beer.

I locked my door at night, unlocked it in the morning.

Did the chores I was scheduled to do.

By then it was obvious I was never going home.

Or maybe even getting up again.

5:20 A.M.

At first light I can see out the window. It's an odd angle, from the floor, a view of eaves and gutters and under-roofs, a line of grimy flats. Pink-green. Orange-blue. A love-me trim. For half a block, I can see the gauze of curtains, tops of heads behind them, peering out for the mail or the bus or someone vaguely familiar to wave to. I can see the reflection of televisions, hosts and scores and a cartoon ferret distended across a white plaster ceiling. The horns of insulted cabs play call and response. A traffic light changes too quickly.

Brake, curse, a trail of weary threats.

Upstairs, a faucet turning.

Someone coughs, three times.

If you lie and watch long enough, along the curving ridge of Guerrero Street, every description will have an action to complement it. Every reason will have a reason not to.

Soon, Johnny will come in with breakfast on a tray.

Thursday will be Friday and the morning's noises, laughter, anger, orgasm, will thrum along my spine.

Welcome Thieves

There's a new pool hall just off campus. The door guy has a shaved head, warns Adam to take it easy on the cues and then keeps his change.

"Don't sweat it," the cocktail girl says. "He just got out of prison."

Adam pretends to line up a shot, checks her out. Nerd glasses, no tats, cheap silver rings on every finger.

"Me too. We were probably on the same tier."

"You hang with the Aryans?"

"Muslim Brotherhood."

"What you in for?"

"That's a question can get you shanked."

"C'mon. Ponzi scheme?"

"Mann Act."

She laughs. Adam drops a twenty on her tray.

"What happens if I order a drink?"

"I'll bring it."

"What if I don't tip?"

"You will."

"What's your name?"

"Eve."

On Friday they go see a saxophone player and slam tequila, end up in the corner of a dumpy Mission bar, kiss along with the beat and through the changes. Adam winds his hand inside Eve's skirt, plays with the elastic band of her underwear, her uniform being just about the cutest thing in town—black top, black mini, HI, I'M YOUR SERVER!

People try to flag them, order drinks. It's a kick.

And then it's a month.

And they still don't hate each other yet.

Eve's just south of pretty, hair cut in an architectural sweep, silver hoops and red cowboy boots. Foot up on the rail, knocking them back. She exudes a complete lack of bullshit, guys staring into their ice thinking how lucky Adam is, thinking screw the models and heiresses, a girl who can laugh deep and raw, who can incorrectly quote Proust while slamming a double Jim Beam and then lean across the felt for a killer cross-side bank, is almost certainly worth her weight in pure uncut Turkish hashish.

"Give me a sense of humor over chocolate and flowers,"

Eve says, racking the balls after another win. "Any day of the week."

Dudes along the rail laugh, raise their drinks.

"Tonight we will not sleep on the petals of the roses I will never buy you," Adam whispers, kisses behind her ear.

THERE ARE MATINEES. Eve likes them dim, with rubber monsters. Adam is a sucker for subtitles. They trade music. Dissonant classical. Nina Simone. Mountain with Leslie West. They talk politics, talk literature, declare the ironic cowardly on a blanket in her blanket-sized backyard, mojitos and carrot sticks and a Dixie cup of ranch dressing.

Eve bats her eyelashes.

"Well, should we go upstairs?"

They've been chaste so far. Why? Because it's hard work. Because it's more fun to be exasperated, pant in the hallway, force each other to unlatch and say goodnight. Just like their parents had to. Like their parents' parents. Let other people give in to carnal stupidity, the ease of obviousness, all the way home on a bus full of gangbangers like he just shoplifted a crow bar.

When it finally happens it will be a thing of beauty, a revelation.

Adam rolls in the grass, pretends to consider.

"Yeah, okay."

Eve's apartment is full of fem textbooks, Steinems and Dworkins and Paglias. She spells women *womyn*, worships

PJ Harvey, breathes a combo of dirty and *oh, darling* into his ear, switches between position and era and arbitrary gender designation.

No one has ever called Adam a filthy dyke before.

Afterward Eve sits up and tells him they didn't just fuck.

"We didn't?"

"I enveloped you. There's a difference."

He pops in a new disc, Dolly's *The Bargain Store*, gets up and makes a pair of G&Ts. They play chess naked in the kitchen, stick to the seats while Adam demolishes Eve's advance of unprotected pawns.

"Listen, I think we should make it official."

"What, like a referee?"

"I think we should be committed."

"What, like Bellevue?"

Adam bites his tongue. Literally. It hurts.

"No, like boyfriend and girlfriend."

"Sorry pal, but you can take that patriarchy and bake it."

He brings out the king's horse, forks her rook. "Why, you want to see other people?"

She considers her position, doomed. "I want to not be interested in your opinion if I do."

A fly circles in front of the stove, bobs and weaves. Adam reaches out.

"Got it."

"Not a chance."

"You think I'm lying, open your mouth."

"Fuck that."

He holds out his fist. "Scared?"

Eve shows molar. He presses his hand to her lips. The fly zips in. She runs to the sink, gags and spits.

Not gloating seems cooler, so Adam mixes another drink, heavy on the G, light on the T. She grabs his shoulder from behind, wrenches him to the floor. The drink spills, ice rattling into the corners.

Eve straddles Adam, pins his arms beneath her knees.

"Fine. We're a couple."

"Wait, really?"

"Really."

She sticks out her tongue.

He bites it.

Dear Gabriel,

It's the best of times and the slightly less best of times. Actually, I'm in sort of a bind here. I'd tell you all about it except then you'd be an accessory and when I get squeezed by the Feds you'll be the first one I rat out. I'm not proud of my weaknesses, but at least I know what they are. Hey, has your mom talked you into joining the Peace Corps yet? If so, I say don't sweat the grades. Party with your friends before it's too late and you're digging a well in Gambia.

Love, Uncle Adam

He wakes up, scared.

There's a noise at the door. After a while it goes away.

For weeks Adam has been pretending everything's fine. No one wants a boyfriend with baggage, right? But, seriously, shit is getting real.

If Adam had just moved into a different building he would never have met the guy across the hall. Bruce Parsley. Tall, bald hustler in a floppy Gilligan hat. Has PARSE tattooed on his neck and when you meet him points to it and goes, "Call me Parse." Bruce Parsley spends every afternoon in the driveway under a beach umbrella. With a cooler and a tracksuit. Dudes walk by and slap five with folded twenties in their palm, walk off with merchandise. Different stuff, depends on the day. Only thing Parse doesn't move is drugs. He points to a needle and a happy-faced spoon tattooed on his arm, "I don't move no drugs."

If Adam had just grabbed that studio in Piedmont, he never would have opened his yap, bragged that he was all about business, a killer salesman, crushed the numbers on the big board in the back room at Comp-U City, lit blunts with Benjamins, could talk an Eskimo into a crate of seal jelly, could get an Arab to buy rubbers packed with sand.

"It's not what you study, it's how you use it on the street."

Bruce Parsley grinned. "That so?"

"Hell, yeah," Adam said, wanting to be a tough guy without the balls to step back and laugh, *Hey, man, forget it, I'm full of shit.*

And now Bruce Parsley is righteously pissed. Could be for any number of slights or business aggravations, but probably rooted in the fact that he fronted Adam nine Samsung

9s in a plastic bag, the ones with the retina display and voice-activated package, handed them over like, "You know what this means, right?"

"Definitely."

"You know I know where you live, right?"

"Of course."

Bruce Parsley nodded, popped a can of Old Mil with his thumb.

"Don't fuck with me son, I go ten deep."

Adam immediately lined up a buyer for all the units at a nice profit, waited down at the waiting spot. But the rich prep kids his friend had vouched for turned out to be four speed-metals in a roofer's truck. They revved over, wiry and feral, snatched the bag, and sped away.

Now Adam practically has to sneak into his own place, phone buzzing twice an hour, texts piling up.

> BParse69: Adam, this ain't no LOL. Need units or cash asap

> BParse69: Adam, hounds r comin if u don respnd 2day

> BParse69: Adam u r so dead. K?

Eve rolls over, bad breath. But the good kind. Sour apple. She's gorgeous, half-awake, messy hair and the sort of hangover eyes stylists spend hours faking on models. Adam's throat constricts. From hyperbole? Okay, she's not gorgeous. But for him? Perfect. Is he so freaking lucky? He is.

"Morning."

"Hey."

Adam gets up and starts an omelet, sautées onions and peppers before realizing there are no eggs, drops the whole steaming mess into the sink.

Eve takes a thunderous piss, sits at the kitchen island in nothing but boxers.

"Listen, we need to talk."

Adam prays not pregnant, but if so resolves to handle it way cooler this time.

"Sure. What about?"

"In three days my sister's getting married."

He almost tears up with relief.

"Hey, that's great."

"Yeah. Except for the part where I so fucking hate her. Like, ten years and eleven thousand dollars worth of therapy later, our drama is even less resolved."

"What about your parents?"

"Don't get mad, I was totally gonna tell you. Dead. Cessna. Tried to land in a cornfield. Was saving the story for a night we had some wine and I felt like crying. Anyway, I get a call yesterday, Uncle Benny is drunk and going on about how I have to come. He keeps saying you're a *brides*maid. You'll *regret* it. *Trust* me on this."

"Wait, you're Jewish?"

"No. Why?"

"Um, the cadence?"

"Sorry, Lutheran."

"Anyway, Uncle Benny is?"

"Dad's brother. Sort of takes care of us now. You ever heard of Winter Kills?"

"Sure."

Eve pretends to look at the watch she's not wearing, taps the imaginary face.

"Let it sink in a minute."

He does. Nothing's there. Until it is.

"Wait, your uncle is *Benny Winters*?"

"I mean, yeah."

Winter Kills used to make upper-crusty sportswear that somehow blew up with the lower crust, b-boys and corner loungers suddenly wearing five-hundred-dollar windbreakers and shooting each other over gold deck shoes. There were a few lawsuits. Poor PR decisions. Eventually the Internet banded together and wrote them off as a modern corporate plantation. Protests, broken windows, million-lounger marches. So Winter Kills shuttered for a year and rebranded, changed the name to Welcome Thieves. Opened again with leather and fringe. Choke chains and biker boots. Edible gag balls. It was so weird it worked. So stupid it was brilliant. Now they're bigger than ever.

"Why didn't you tell me?"

"Don't get excited, Uncle Benny's got cement pockets. But he is offering two plane tickets. Plus a hotel room."

Adam imagines standing next to the guy with a drink, turning on the charm. Discussing inventory, capital. Labor relations. CEO shit. Totally not bringing up Indonesian sweatshops or child labor, even just to be like, *What else would those fucking kids do?* Bottom line, Adam has legit ideas. Good ones. A dating app for strippers called Euphemism. Dental house calls. A brand of pork soda called Porksoda. He just needs a mentor. An investor. Any of the *-estors*.

But he's smart enough to take his enthusiasm and bake it.

"So you want me to come. Like, as your boyfriend."

"As my amanuensis."

"I totally know what that means. I just forget right now."

"It means you look good in a tux so all my aunts don't waste calories wondering am I a disciple of Sappho."

"That's a Lesbos reference, right? As in Isle of?"

Eve nods in a way that says she loves that he's following along, has a foot in the game.

"But I don't have a tux."

"Who wears a tux?"

"I don't have a suit."

"You got pants?"

He looks down.

"Yeah."

"Listen, if you're not up to it, I have other candidates."

There's a banging at the door. The new steel hasps are tested. The banging gets louder, loudest, goes away.

"Okay, I'm in."

"Why are you whispering?"

"I'm not."

"Are you sure you can afford to miss a week of classes?"

Adam's major is Trend Creation. It's even dumber than it

sounds. The Internet is already one giant pop-up ad. Movies are two reels of product placement with the occasional actor. All modern relationships are basically people holding hands in outdoor tubs, looking at a sunset and waiting for the Cialis to take hold. There's not a single person left on the planet with spare mental territory for things they actually want. Adam knows he should switch to a hot new discipline, like deprogramming. His very best idea: raise cash to build the Paleo Existence, a theme park in Wyoming filled with dank caves, bison fur skirts, and animatronic sabertooths. Unloose modern hunter-gatherers in a pristine environment surrounded by electric fences. Charge bearded hipsters two hundred for a bag of salt, five for a stone knife and a torch. Let them get their serious *homo-habilis* on for a few weeks, cudgel and hair-drag, make new gods of the stars.

"Yeah, I'm pretty sure I can."

"Good, because there's one other problem."

Okay, now it's definitely pregnant.

"What?"

"I don't fly."

"Don't?"

"Won't. Ever."

"So we have to drive?"

"Yup."

"Where is it?"

"The wedding?"

"No, the circumcision."

"You ever heard of Vegas?"

Dear Gabriel,

People need water to survive. Which is a strange thing, since people are mostly made of water to begin with. Although some scientists, one Lama, and a couple hippies think we're made of dark matter. Which is also a strange thing, because we're not sure what dark matter is, or if it even exists. Which means we're mostly made up of conjecture. We are walking theories. Except for people who can't walk. Or theorize. Don't ever do drugs, Gabriel. Although, when your grandmother told me not to do drugs, I went right out and immediately did drugs. So forget I said anything. You'll do whatever the hell you want to in the end. Dark matter always does.

Love, Uncle Adam

He hits a used car lot deep in the Oakland wasteland, buys an '89 Taurus for three hundred bucks. Cigarette burns across the dash, a sheen of previous drivers you couldn't disinfect with kerosene. Then forges notes to each of his professors alluding to something undiagnosed, but likely contagious. Finally wins a hundred in gas money hustling lames at nine ball, packs a duffel, tiptoes past Bruce Parsley's door.

Beep-beep-ba-beep.

Eve hops in the passenger side, looks hot, black bodysuit and red lips, turns the radio to NPR. A man who sounds like a receding hairline discusses the Egyptian situation. Then an interview with John Updike's mistress, who insists Rabbit was a lousy lay.

"She sounds like fun."

"Chick's a human stain."

"That's a Roth joke, right? 'Cause they're, like, similarly misogynistic in style?"

Eve leans over and kisses him, buckles his seatbelt and then hers.

They take side streets to the bridge, find a space in the capillary action, one honking Prius after another. Eve grabs her bag, a vintage pink oval Tina Marie probably once hauled around Malibu. She finds a cellophane, dabs at her nose. Adam doesn't like coke but is a firm believer that things he doesn't like and what anyone else might need to make it through another day on this depressing fuckhead of a planet are two entirely different propositions. Or at least he's said that in bars sometimes. To girls. It usually works.

Eve cracks a textbook, flips pages.

"Wait, are you serious?"

"I have a paper due when we get back."

"On obsessive behavior?"

She gives him the finger, speed-reads aloud. Apparently matriarchal societies flourished before the time of Jesus but had been branded heretics by early Christians. In India, women burned themselves on pyres when their husbands died, in a custom called suttee. There's a whole chapter on Madonna, and another, even longer one, on the less-appreciated Brontë.

Then it's midnight and they're somewhere south of L.A. Adam is pretty sure he should have cut east at some point. There's a sign for an all-night diner.

"Hungry?"

"Starving."

The place is packed, truckers, bartenders just off shift. Suspenders and denim. Horsetail wreaths and George Jones framed in charcoal. The waitress is cute in her little outfit, white nylons. Sort of a punky haircut, short, uneven.

"We're not really handicapped," Eve tells her, points to the Taurus.

"Don't worry about it. Only one who ever parks in that spot is the cook, unless you count fat a handicap."

Eve orders eggs, pancakes, bacon, home fries, coffee, bagel, sweet roll, sausage, potatoes, rye toast, wheat toast, Kix, jelly.

Adam's phone buzzes.

BParse69: In yr apartment right now.

BParse69: Taking shit on yr bed. Dude u ever heard of thread count?

BParse69: Hope nothing important on this comp u ter.

"I'm gonna go find a sports section."

Eve makes a face.

"You hate sports."

"I meant world news."

The little convenience store is closed. He leaves some dimes on top of a stack of bound *Clarion-Ledger*s, sees the Taurus has a ticket beneath the wiper.

"Raw luck," says a guy smoking two Winstons at once.

"I don't believe in luck."

"What do you believe in?"

"Jinxes."

The guy laughs. "Where y'all headed?"

"Dollywood."

"In that piece of shit?"

"It's a classic. There's a monster under the hood."

Eve knuckles the other side the window, holds up a ham steak dripping with syrup.

"Wife's sure in a hurry."

"Nah, she just knows I like it with the bone in."

The guy nods, walks to his car. Adam dabs his underarms with the ticket, begins to sing, "We afraid to live, afraid of dyin', afraid to love the one we love, 'cause you know they surely lying."

THE SUN COMES up in the fast lane, confirms that Rancho Cucamonga is indeed grim as fuck. Same with San Bernardino.

"Trend Create it for me," Eve says, taking in the Taco Locos and nail salons. "Sell me on this shit."

Adam clears his throat.

"Four lanes became three lanes became two. Everything got flat. There were triple the advertisements for pie. Patches of fur lay redly across the double yellows, dead grackles strung like cursive from post to post. Modern living at its finest, a poetry of fake adobe, casual decay, and easy access to the highway of your dreams. Call Adam for details."

"Shit, you're good," Eve says, and then falls asleep with her head on the dash. He taps the speedometer, which continues not to work, mashes the pedal to the floor. A few hours later they ease into the lot of Uncle Benny's hotel. It's nowhere close to the strip, out in endless sprawl of shuttered schools and red clay yards.

"Can I help you?" the clerk asks.

"Probably not, but we'll take a room anyhow."

The elevator rises. They unpack, have a few drinks.

"Let's watch porn," Eve says.

"Really?"

"Quick, before I change my mind."

Adam dials it up, throws her on the quilt, takes her face in his hands and stares meaningfully.

Eve yawns.

He kisses her ankles, the aristocratic tilt of her neck, closely admires the way her pubic hair forms an elegant Helvetica *V*, a wily lure furrowed into tight little curls. She stops yawning, kisses him back. They are slow and considered, thighs tense, strangers on a guided tour in the south of France who slip away with half a bottle of wine and a blanket, kill the afternoon fumbling all over each other under the looming Provençal vines.

Or maybe that's just the plot of the movie.

In the end it's a good one, definitely worth $29.95.

THE CLOCK RADIO BUZZES. Eve gets up and showers, goes to town on the free soaps and lotions. Adam sits at the tiny desk, turns over the cover of *The Man with the Golden Arm*, and affixes a stamp.

Dear Gabriel,

Here I am in Las Vegas, which some people call Lost Vegas and other people call Hell on Earth. I'm going to a wedding tomorrow. Weddings can be fun, but mostly I think if you were here, you'd wish you weren't. When you're eighteen I'm going to drive by in a ~~stolen~~ big ole truck and take you on a ~~roadie~~ short ride. We'll go backpacking in Idaho and live off the land for a while and ~~eat bugs like men~~ camp responsibly according to established forest service regulations. Also, we'll drink ~~whiskey~~ milk and meet ~~girl backpackers~~ a couple of buddies and go ~~skinny-dipping~~ home at midnight. But don't tell your mom that.

Love, Uncle Adam

"What are you writing?"

"Nothing."

Eve holds out her arms, spins. She's in a tiny black bikini, red lips, sandals. Her body is a monument to sleek engineering, to experimental hydraulics and efficient design.

"You look ridiculously hot, but I'm pretty sure there's no pool here."

"Put on your trunks. We're hitting the beach."

"Sounds fun and all, but I'm pretty sure we're in the middle of the desert."

"Did you happen to notice that big metal shed when we drove in?"

"Yeah."

"Put on your trunks."

THE HANGER'S MASSIVE, the kind they park blimps in. The sign says CALIFORNIA DREAMIN: AN IMMERSION. Two registers, a turnstile, eighty a ticket.

The atrium is all glass, huge sun lamps bolted to ceiling rafters. The floor is covered with metric tons of sand. A giant machine slides back and forth along the far wall, like a printer cartridge, producing sets of waves, three-footers at least. They break, get sucked back, roll in again. The beach is packed with families and umbrellas, floats and balls and shovels.

"You've got to be kidding," Adam says.

"I know. Isn't it awesome?"

They walk down to the water, feet in the surf. Eve's bikini is smaller than the price tag still clipped to it. Frat dudes swivel their necks, test out their baritones. Eve lays down a blanket, arranges creams and aloes and water and books and sunglasses. She puts on a cowboy hat made of straw, the kind men who pick artichokes might wear on a Saturday night in Berdoo.

"Incoming," Adam says, as one of the frat boys strolls over, frozen drink in a plastic tube, cheap wrap-around shades and a complete lack of belly. His bright orange shorts have a WEL-COME THIEVES logo across the hem.

"What's up, bro?"

Adam can't process the *bro*, let alone respond. A devastating punch wells in the coiled spring of his filmic imagination.

"So me and my boys were wondering if y'all were just friends. Like maybe beach pals or whatever?"

The other guys laugh their asses off, wrestle and pound sand.

Eve rises on one elbow, points at Adam. "This here is my cousin Biebs."

Adam knows he's supposed to play along, but hates this sort of meta shit. Acting like there's a camera just out of frame. No one sure who the joke is on, but three-to-one it's not them.

"Cool. So you and Biebs got plans tonight? Or maybe just you?"

"I bet there's a killer party," Eve says. "I bet you know just where it is."

"Damn straight."

"How about a club? A hot new club and you're besties with the door guy?"

"True. Also very true."

"You going somewhere, Biebs?" Eve asks.

Adam walks down to the water and hikes the length of the beach, pokes around the dunes for a while. Some kids are making out. Others smoke dope hunkered in the vinyl grass. He finds a quiet spot to dig in his toes, pulls out the cover of Theodore Sturgeon's *Killdozer!* and affixes a stamp.

Dear Gabriel,

I want to write a poetry collection, but before I get busy with the stanzas and pentameter and shit, I need a killer title. Which do you think is best?

1. Storming the Battlements, Battling the Stormaments

2. A Most Contemptible Contretemps

3. Six Thieves for Seven Dollars

Adam started with the postcards when Gabriel was eight and his sister's husband left her.

"For, can you believe it, some *Indian* chick?"

"You mean like Calcutta or Trail of Tears?"

"Seriously," Beth said. "Gabriel needs a man in his life."

"Try a bar. Wear something low-cut."

"He's started lighting things on fire. They caught him at school burning a desk. And eating the lining of someone's jacket."

"Hey, I'm sorry."

"Great, thanks. That's already made a huge difference."

Adam pictured himself at Gabriel's age, the smirking turd he'd been. "I'll email him, Beth. How about that? Or we can FaceTime. You have a computer, right?"

"He already spends about fourteen hours a day online. Don't you think that's part of the problem?"

"How the hell would I know?"

"Exactly, Adam. How would you?"

He and Beth had never been close, two years apart, different mothers, a state-to-state traipse all through high school as their father chased jobs that more accurately reflected his skill set, which in the end meant running a boutique hotel that offered continental breakfast, free cable, amd fabulous duvets.

"Fine. Listen, I'll think of something, okay?"

The next day Adam was in a used bookstore, leafing

through a stack of old pulps, like *Ladies in Hades* and *Pickup on Sin Street*. The art was lurid. Ridiculous. Also completely excellent. Almost pretechnology. An admission that we were all lonely and furtive, that at one time even grown men lacked access to the rudiments of self-pleasure.

He tore away the cover of *She Was a Shark!* and put it back on the shelf. The cashier continued to text. So he tore two more.

"Gabriel loves them," Beth reported. "Honestly, Adam? It's genius. Without the actual book, there's, like, this weird liberation. He tacks each cover to the wall above his bed. Stares for hours. Makes up his own plots to fit the titles. I had no idea he was so imaginative."

Adam became the scourge of East Bay indies, perfected a rip-disguising cough. Clerks hovered, oblivious, as he liberated Jim Thompson and Stanislaw Lem, Hubert Selby and Iceberg Slim. He felt empathy for the little paperbacks, stripped and vulnerable, spines bare and raw.

But not enough to stop.

At first he had no clue what to write. *How are your classes?* Or *Playing any sports at school?* But that got boring almost immediately. Plus, Adam remembered how much he hated being asked that sort of thing. In the end, he just let the pen decide. Gabriel never responded, instinctively knowing that wasn't part of the deal.

Killdozer! catches a raindrop. And then two. The ink starts to run. Adam looks up, figures it has to be condensation from one of the fans, but lifeguards blow their whistles and yell as ominous clouds gather, begin to roll in. Of course they're CGI, projected on a screen, but it's amazingly convincing. *Everyone out! Now!* Some people are confused, but most play along, gather their kids, slap five. A chain-link fence is rolled in front of the water, which begins to seethe and churn. In the distance lightning crackles, lances down from ceiling to breaker. Waves crash against the shore, spend themselves in purple foam, scalded bubbles rising from fake clams.

Children laugh and clap, delighted.

A rubber whale breaches. More applause. Dolphins frolic, their oddly human laughter echoing through the sound system. What's probably the *Titanic* heads toward what's probably an iceberg.

Fuck it.

Adam lopes past the guards, in one motion scales the links, tosses himself over.

"Hey! Hey, you!"

He ankles through the chop. The water is cold. Or maybe that's another effect. There are a volley of whistles, a flickering alarm. Adam is tossed around, abraded by foam rocks, comes up spuming for breath. People angle their phones, shoot video. A set of waves pounds by like freezers tumbling from a truck on the highway.

He has no choice but to dive beneath or take the full brunt.

The first twenty seconds are the worst, panicwise. And then things slow down. Adam watches schools of tiny fish linger and dart in unison. They must be real. Or maybe holograms? Tiny chips shoved into rubber fins? There's a manta ray far below, and possibly a tiger shark circling above, which fits nicely with the cheap high from oxygen depletion.

Adam gets seriously Zen, figures the ocean will decide what the ocean will decide.

Even if it's run by a shelf of Pentium IIIs.

"Get up," Eve says for the third time, presses her thumb into Adam's forehead. "We need to get fitted."

He's waterlogged and groggy. The elevator dings. There's the gentle lilt of Spanish from maids in the hall. Across his shoulders are bruises shaped like squid, or possibly the grip of unamused lifeguards.

"Wait, why again?"

"Oh, I dunno," Eve says, her voice knitting together the spine of their first real fight. "Because you can't go to the wedding in a towel?"

It's raining hard. Almost no one else is out on the road. The Taurus slides instead of rolls, shudders deeply at each red light.

"Sorry," Eve says.

"About what?"

"Talking to that guy."

"What guy?"

"At the beach."

"What beach?"

She puts her hand over his, locks fingers.

They pass a Welcome Thieves billboard featuring a kid in tight white briefs. A centurion offers him a grape from the tip of his spear, while a woman behind them lashes two blind stallions with a garden hose.

The store is cramped, windows fogged. Big-haired girls paw through racks of prom dresses while their mothers wait. Eve comes out of the changing room in a hideous flesh-colored gown, holding her breath.

"How do I look?"

Adam stands on a wooden box while a tiny man with a gray Afro and a mouthful of pins adjusts his cuffs. The prom girls stop nattering and stare. The cashier stares. The stock boys rub their hairless cheeks and do a credible job of pretending not to stare.

"Well?"

Eve is flushed, hair swept back, delicate arms and shoulders lending architecture to the dress. She's in heels, lips red, nails pink. A woman. A queen. The reason Pericles sacked Delphi, that all of Thrace burned.

"Gorgeous," Adam says.

"Really?"

She curtsies, spins the hem, absolutely owns that rag.

"I can't believe you're my date. Shit, I can't believe I'm yours."

Eve bites her lip, slides behind a curtain. One of the prom girls bursts into tears. The rest take turns comforting her, peek at Adam through the racks.

"Boy, I sure figured you wrong," the tailor says, looking up over his glasses.

"Huh?"

"Had you down for a wise-ass comment. Woulda bet the house you messed that up. And then *bam*, my man comes through. Tell you the truth, that's the first time I been surprised since O.J."

THEY'RE LATE. EVE gives him a kiss, hustles away while he finds a parking spot. Adam sits alone in the back row. The church feels more like a casino. He keeps expecting triple cherries to hit, someone's uncle about to shake twelve grand loose from a pew. The priest drones on for a while. Mostly about how it's better if you're good to each other. How it really is preferable if you don't have sex with your wife's best friend, or spend the house fund on meth. Then it's Latin, Latin, Latin.

Eve stands on the podium, chin up, flanked by lesser women drowning in frills and lace.

It's impossible not to be proud.

Also, continuously buzzed.

BParse69: Yr mother's name is Janet, right? Lives on Peach Tree Lane?

BParse69: Whoze this cute chick in all the pics? Can u txt me her #?

BParse69: Bunch of hard pipe-hitters I know jus cleaned out yr place.

After the ceremony, Eve boards a van with the wedding party. Adam follows with some rowdy Welcome Thieves employees. There's talk about the bride (saddled), Uncle Benny (asshole), gowns (dreadful), stock options (plummeting), and attendance (mandatory). They cross town, the reception in a parking lot next to a WT distribution center. A huge pin-striped awning sits in the middle of the tarmac, AstroTurf laid out in squares. On the far stage the band struggles through a Billy Joel cover, power cutting in and out. Every thirty seconds the rain produces a series of electronic squalls that warn of undue voltage and massive equipment death.

"Unbelievable," the man next to Adam says, dabbing at his suit. "Winters is such a cheap fuck."

There's a grumbling assent. Guests hold papers over their heads, newsprint running under cuffs. Wives and dates stumble in heels while a priest tries to protect the elderly with a broken umbrella. They finally make it under the awning but it's only dry in the center. Guests push together like encounter therapy, bartenders and caterers stuck on the fringe, miserable, wiping droplets of water from each other's chins.

Adam finds himself in the receiving line. The groom has mirrored Oakleys and sideburns, flecks of powder dusting his left nostril. He shakes Adam's hand, says it's awesome to see him again.

"That's cool. Except we've never met."

"Who you here with again?"

"Eve."

The groom shakes his head.

"Oh, dude. Oh, man."

"Yeah."

"You fucker."

"Yeah."

He's passed off to Eve's sister. It's pretty clear why they don't get along. She's got the bones of a big girl, impossibly thin, looks like a car fire, flushed, pink, ravenous. Like she could never get drunk enough, but you wouldn't know, because you'd already be blacked out behind the fridge. She pulls Adam into a hug, which gives him a view of the tattoo between her shoulder blades, Bettie Page firing a machine gun made from a decomposed leg.

An artist. He'd put money on performances that involve food.

"Come find me later," she whispers. "Let's dance."

"Definitely," Adam says, hits the bar, orders a G&T that's 70 percent rainwater.

"Listen, thanks for coming," Benny Winters says, grabs his shoulder exactly where the lifeguard did. Uncle Benny has silver eyebrows and Gatsby hair, smells like cologne made from orphans' tears.

"Glad to be here."

"Who are you again?"

"Only the guy who's gonna marry your other niece."

Uncle Benny nods, half smiles. His indifference is maddening, lips pursed like Adam isn't even worth the refutation. Or congratulations.

"So I guess once I'm family I'll start at Welcome Thieves."

"I see."

"Yeah, I'll work my way into your confidence over a meteoric decade's rise, all the while secretly engineering a board insurrection that leaves you penniless."

Uncle Benny cocks his head, shrugs.

"Under my stewardship, the company will morph into providing immersive wilderness experiences in Wyoming. You're probably not hip to the whole Paleo thing, but it'll be like printing twenties in the basement."

"Sure," Uncle Benny says.

"The thing is, I'm not gonna do all that for the cash. Or even Eve. Basically, you and your sweatshop thongs have made the world a tackier, more imbecilic place. Someone has to blow the whistle. Even if just for karma's sake. Which, honestly, I don't even believe in. But that just proves my point."

Uncle Benny muses, probably about whether or not to signal one of the security types milling by the exit. Then he cocks his head, pulls a Bluetooth from his other ear.

"Excuse me. Emergency in Hong Kong. What were you saying?"

Adam points to the awning, which sags and billows in turn.

"Just that I'm Fred, your tent rep. This here's our top model."

Uncle Benny eyes the fabric like a pro.

"Well, I guess this deluge isn't your fault."

"No sir. If you care to re-examine the fine print in your contract, we are not responsible for torrents, spates, or acts of God."

Uncle Benny slips a fifty into Adam's top pocket, and then they watch people dance. Some are really good. Others bumble around, drunk or clumsy or just out of practice. The groom flails maniacally, cummerbund undone and stuck into his belt like a tail. He twirls an ancient woman in black wool. Adam fears for her bones, forced to clack knees to the swollen chorus of "Hungry Like the Wolf."

And then there's a bang, the sound of wet flesh coming together by the ladies' room.

"Uh-oh," Uncle Benny says, jogs toward the crowd already gathering around Eve and her sister, who are nose to nose.

Adam heads out into the rain, follows a wash of runoff down to the oddly precise line where the fake grass ends and the cactus begins. Bones of a million animals, lizards, birds, and armadillos rise from the sand, newly exposed and glistening. He remembers the book covers too late, pulls them from his inside pocket in sections, wet and unintelligible.

After a while, Eve's hand slips into his.

"Everything okay?"

"It is now. I should pull her hair more often."

"I think Benny really likes me."

"Doubt it."

"How come?"

"He doesn't even like himself."

"What a backward way to see the world."

They kiss while looking out over the desert floor, which in the pounding rain could be the Pacific, or even Mars.

Dear Gabriel,

We may all drown here. It's becoming biblical, not necessarily the best omen for a wedding day. The word *antediluvian* means "before the flood," as in pre-Noah. You know, the guy and his Ark? Two of every animal, brides and grooms. Here, the groom is working his way through a carton of no filters. You don't smoke, do you? Get it out of your system now, if you have to, while your organs are still resilient.

Well, I got nothing to go home to now. I'm a man without a campus or country. Which would be a good title for a book but a bad line for a headstone.

Anyway, I guess I'll try somewhere new. Here? There? Who cares? All you really need in life is one friend. I have one friend. Her name is Eve. Go ahead and make your jokes, get them out of the way. Adam and Eve. Lucy and Ricky. Kanye and tits. Sometimes perfect symmetry portends unearned privilege and random birth defects, but in our case, perfect, uncut kismet.

Hey, maybe this summer we can take you to a movie, something with monsters but no guns. Or we can all go get drunk. Get a bottle of wine and park out by the airport and watch the planes come in.

Gabriel, it's vital to remember that there's absolutely nothing you couldn't take 80 percent less seriously.

Except possibly generalized statements involving percentages.

I know this is too wet to read, but, really, that just proves my point.

Love, Uncle Adam

Acknowledgments

The author would like to thank the many people who at one time or another read various incarnations of these stories, and provided invaluable support and perspective along the way:

Kristine Serio, Liesl Wilkie, Christian Bauer, Cari Phillips, Diana Spechler (look her up, read her books), Jillian Smith, D. B. Miller (look her up, read her articles), Greg Olear (look him up, read his articles and books), Martha Brockenbrough (look her up, buy it all), Hank Cherry (drool over his photographs), Antonia Crane (killer memoir), Garth Stein (you're halfway through it now), and Jonathan Evison (ignore him). Also, Joe Daly, Kevin Emerson, Noël Casiano, Larry Benner, Janet Steen, Maria Behan, Hank Kyburg, Matty "Clum" Heller, and Stella.

My fabulous agent, Jennifer de la Fuente, and the sometimes Cormac-like road we traveled together at Fountain Literary.

Angelo Gianni for Full Visual Support.

The editors of all the journals who published earlier, vastly inferior versions of many of these stories. Support lit journals! You don't even have to read them: Pay the cover price and hand the copy to someone on the street. Buy a subscription and donate it to the library. Send them a blank check and a box of Red Vines.

Dark Coast Press for refusing to acquire this manuscript; Aaron and Jarret for not putting it out far too soon and entirely unready; hero figures in the first chapter of the book that Should Never Have Been.

Certain cafés where sections of these stories were written, redlined, and lashed together again: Bauhaus, Caffe Ladro, Fremont Coffee Company, Stone Way Cafe, and Uptown Espresso.

For "Nick in Nine (9) Movements," Mike Nesi, Adam Sandone, Dave Renz, and P. J. Casey. For "All Dreams Are Night Dreams," Johnny Minton and just another night in Vegas. For "Hey Monkey Chow," the sad and disturbing case of St. James Davis, attacked by his pet chimpanzee in 2005, and the *San Francisco Chronicle* article that described it. For "And Now Let's Have Some Fun," the insanity of UFC 3, caught late at night and totally at random, but mostly for a cross-dragging Kimo. For "Base Omega Has Twelve Dictates," Ricardo Perez and his unwavering love of two toss-off paragraphs that I finally broke down and turned into a story. For "Exposure," if you don't remember being there, you weren't there.

A very great thanks to everyone at Algonquin, including Elisabeth Scharlatt, Brunson Hoole, Craig Popelars, Lauren Moseley, Kelly Clark Policelli, Debra Linn, Ina Stern, Emma Boyer, Brooke Csuka, Anne Winslow, and Steve Godwin.

And especially Chuck Adams, for his wit, style, and editorial grace—but mostly for believing in this collection from the very beginning.